Markinfield Addey

**The Life and Military Career of Thomas Jonathan Jackson**

Markinfield Addey

**The Life and Military Career of Thomas Jonathan Jackson**

ISBN/EAN: 9783337016913

Printed in Europe, USA, Canada, Australia, Japan

Cover: Foto ©Raphael Reischuk / pixelio.de

More available books at **www.hansebooks.com**

*"STONEWALL JACKSON."*

THE

# LIFE AND MILITARY CAREER

OF

# THOMAS JONATHAN JACKSON,

LIEUTENANT-GENERAL IN THE CONFEDERATE ARMY.

BY

## MARKINFIELD ADDEY.

WITH A PORTRAIT.

NEW-YORK:
CHARLES T. EVANS.
448 Broadway.

1863.

JOHN A. GRAY & GREEN,
*Printers, Stereotypers, and Binders,*
Cor. of Frankfort and Jacob Sts.,
FIRE-PROOF BUILDINGS.

# To the Brave,

WITHOUT DISTINCTION OF COUNTRY OR CLIME,

THIS STORY OF VALOROUS DEEDS

IS DEDICATED.

# PREFACE.

THE following Biographical Sketch is given to the public in obedience to a general desire for information relative to the soldier who has during the past two years occupied so much of the public attention, and has played so important a part in the stirring scenes of the great American Rebellion. The work claims to be a narrative of facts and a detailed description of the leading events in General Jackson's military career—events exhibiting such a high order of military skill, such indomitable energy, and such exalted courage, that they have caused the story of his deeds to travel far and wide, and have stamped his name as being that of the most brilliant commander of the war.

It was on the battle-field that Jackson achieved his renown, and it is to the history of the battles in which he fought that we must naturally look for a record of the most important incidents of his life. In describing these, the author has found it necessary to do so with some degree of completeness, as it was only by following this plan that the importance of Jackson's operations in some particular part of the field, or the full force of one of his celebrated flank movements, could be properly estimated. The main spring or the lever forms but part of the mechanism of a watch, but it is impossible to thoroughly appreciate the importance of either without a study of the whole. The analogy holds good in the principal battles in which Jackson fought. It was almost invariably some well-conceived movement or some sudden dash of his that turned the tide of battle in the Confederate favor, or enabled him to ward off some disastrous blow; but this movement or this dash would be only a part of some prearranged plan, the effect of which would be felt throughout the entire battle-field.

So remarkably successful was Jackson in his peculiar but brilliant style of fighting, that his presence in the combat invariably inspired confidence on one side and dismay on the other, causing him to become the popular hero; and the name of "Stonewall" Jackson to stand as a symbol of victory. He was truly the right arm of the Confederate army, and in the first battle that General Lee fought after his death—the battle of Gettysburg — he was fully able to estimate the loss he had sustained in the death of so distinguished a general.

Not the least important of Jackson's characteristics were his religious and devotional habits. With these he was enabled to imbue those under his command, so that the hearts of officers and men beat and their arms smote in unison. This feeling fired them with zeal for their cause, for to them death had no terrors. Valorous in the highest degree, and audacious without bounds, they rushed headlong into the fight. They thought not of to-morrow, and pined not at the privations which they were often compelled to experience. The devotion of the men to their commander was remarkable. They had every confidence in their leader, and fearlessly and courageously obeyed his every bidding. Jackson's religion taught him to be charitable toward a fallen foe, so that the wounded Federal who fell into his hands was equally cared for as the disabled soldier of his own corps.

The people of the North cannot but honor the noble qualities which existed in one they had so much cause to fear, and at whose hands they so much suffered. Whilst they must ever regret that Jackson, at the period of his doubtings, at the commencement of the Rebellion, should have finally decided to espouse the cause of the South, they cannot decline to pay fitting homage to the memory of one who was so noble in heart and so chivalric in action.

NEW-YORK, *August*, 1863.

# CONTENTS.

## CHAPTER I.

### BEFORE THE REBELLION.

## CHAPTER II.

### THE UPPER POTOMAC.

## CHAPTER III.

### THE BATTLE OF BULL RUN.

## CHAPTER IV.

### WINTER CAMPAIGN ON THE UPPER POTOMAC.

## CHAPTER V.

### THE BATTLE OF WINCHESTER.

## CHAPTER VI.

### CAMPAIGN IN THE VALLEY OF THE SHENANDOAH—RETREAT OF GENERAL BANKS.

## CHAPTER VII.

### VALLEY OF THE SHENANDOAH—FEDERAL PURSUIT OF JACKSON.

## CHAPTER VIII.

### THE SEVEN DAYS' BATTLES BEFORE RICHMOND.

## CHAPTER IX.

### THE CAMPAIGN AGAINST GENERAL POPE.

## CHAPTER X.

### THE INVASION OF MARYLAND.

## CHAPTER XI.

### THE BATTLE OF FREDERICKSBURGH.

## CHAPTER XII.

### THE BATTLE OF CHANCELLORSVILLE.

## CHAPTER XIII.

### LAST MOMENTS AND OBSEQUIES.

## ADDENDA.

### INCIDENTS AND CHARACTERISTICS.

# THE LIFE AND MILITARY CAREER

OF

# LIEUT.-GEN. THOMAS JONATHAN JACKSON.

## CHAPTER I.

### BEFORE THE REBELLION.

His Military Career an Episode in the History of the Rebellion—Compared with the Puritan Leaders of England—Resemblance to Havelock—Northern Appreciation of his Gallantry—Birth and Parentage—Becomes a Student at West-Point—Slow at Study—Futile Attempt to play the Flute—Specimens of Eccentricities—Graduates—Class-Mates—Enters the Army—Proceeds to Mexico—Promoted for his Bravery—Instances of Gallantry—Retires from the Army—Becomes Professor of Mathematics at Lexington, Va.—Escapes Assassination—Married—Becomes a Widower—Married a Second Time.

OF all the names which the surges of the Rebellion have thrown upon the dry sands of history, there is none stands more prominent than does that of THOMAS JONATHAN JACKSON. His military career has been brief, but it has been crowded with startling incidents. It was the career of an enthusiastic, chivalrous, and religious soldier. The story of that career is an episode in the history of the Rebellion,

which is worthy of being separated from the general narrative of the events with which the last two years have
been so prolific.  We therefore now weave together such of
the threads of this hero's life as we are enabled to gather,
and place them before our readers in as perfect a fabric as
possible.

There are many points in Jackson's character which
strongly remind us of Cromwell, and Hampden, and Pym,
and other sturdy and god-fearing Puritans of the time of
England's great Rebellion; but we have cause to regret
that the resemblance is not perfect.  These patriotic Puritans unsheathed the sword to fight the battle of freedom
and of the people against the powerful autocratic element
which in their days ruled the destinies of the British nation;
whilst on the contrary, Jackson in a misguided moment,
was induced to bare his blade for the purpose of wielding
it on the side of a Southern slave-ruling oligarchy, and
against the free people of his own country.

There is much, too, in Jackson's character, that resembles
the pictures which have been drawn of Havelock, who, a
few years ago, rendered his name famous by the brilliancy
of his military performances in India.  Added to a strong
religious feeling which was predominant in the character of
both these Generals, they alike possessed great activity of
mind and fertility of resource, and each exercised over those
under his command such a parental sway, that his entire force
was ever ready to move almost as one man at the beck of its
commander.  This is plainly shown in the celerity of move-

ments and in the long and rapid marches which so mainly
tended to the greatness of their successes. Each considered
that he had a duty to perform — his duty to his country—a
duty, however, which in one case was directed to a sectional part thereof, and against the best interests of the entire nation; and the singleness of purpose of each was so
great, that he removed every obstacle out of the way which
interfered with the proper performance of this duty—never
omitting that greater duty of all men, the duty to his
Maker; never undertaking any enterprise without first invoking the Deity to guide his steps and to bless his en-
deavors with success.

The death of a brave soldier is ever mourned by friend
and foe, and it is honorable to the loyal people of America
that they did not hear of the death of Thomas Jonathan
Jackson without a thrill of emotion passing through their
hearts. Though they viewed him as one of the most dangerous and most resolute of their antagonists, they ever considered him one of the most conscientious and most chival
rous. Though they had reeled under the blows which he
had inflicted upon them, and though they had felt the full
force of the lightnings of battle which he had launched
against them, they knew that the blows had been struck by
a valorous hand, and that it was a noble spirit that had
directed those fearful lightnings.

" War," writes one of our Northern journalists, referring
to Jackson's death, " is never so hateful as when it kills in
men the supremely manlike quality of justice to our ene-

mies; and the spontaneous, irrepressible tribute which rose to all men's lips when they heard that the bravest of the rebel brave had died a soldier's death, was a victory won by the heart and temper of the Northern people, on which the muse of history will linger, perhaps, with something like relief from her sad chronicle of men arrayed for mutual slaughter."

"The Northern people," also says the same writer, "honored in Jackson qualities which the worst cause can not obscure. They respected the sincerity of the man as much as they admired the daring of the soldier. They believed him misled, but they felt that he was no misleader. They lamented in his victories only this, that feats which reflected such renown upon American gallantry should have been performed in a cause so fatal to American hopes; and not even the sense of gain we all must feel in the loss to the rebel hosts of such a captain, can make us stand otherwise than with uncovered heads before the early grave of a heroic chieftain, the example of whose high qualities the truest and most loyal soldier of the Union and the Right may honorably lay to heart."

Thomas Jonathan Jackson was born in Harrison County, Virginia, in January, 1824. He was descended from a mixture of Scotch and Irish blood, and his parents were neither wealthy nor possessed of that aristocratic position which was wont to be the boast of the leading families of the Old Dominion. Still the influence of his family was sufficient to enable them to secure for him admission to the Military Academy at West-Point, to gain which, it is stated, that he travelled on foot from Clarksburgh to Washington.

Jackson entered upon his cadet duties at West-Point in 1842. He was not a remarkably bright pupil; in fact, he was so dull and slow at his studies that it took him three times as long to master his tasks as the average of the other pupils; but what he did learn he learned thoroughly. His disposition was retiring and taciturn, but his face would brighten up with a pleasant smile whenever he entered into conversation. In illustration of the difficulty which young Jackson experienced in learning any thing, we may relate an anecdote told by General Seymour. During the time that the latter and Jackson were both young lieutenants, Seymour amused himself by learning to play the flute, which instrument Jackson also felt an inclination to learn. To accomplish this he went to work with his accustomed vigor and perseverance; but he was never enabled to master even the most simple air, and at last gave up his attentions to the goddess of music, after having for six months unsuccessfully courted her in an attempt to master the first bar of " Love Not." It is evident that he had " no music in himself," and, if Shakspeare is to be believed, he was, in this respect at least, "fit for treasons, stratagems, and spoils."

When Jackson was at West-Point he used to fancy that he suffered from consumption, and that he should die a painful death. In fact, both at this and various other periods of his life, he was afflicted with different forms of hypochondria.

Among the various anecdotes related of his eccentricities during the time of his residence at the Academy, it is stated that he was possessed with the notion that he was in danger of having his limbs paralyzed, and he would pump on his arm for many minutes, counting the strokes, and feeling annoyed beyond measure whenever his companions interrupted him in his count. He was also wont to sit upright at his meals, and had a curious way of holding up his head very straight, whilst his chin would appear as if it were trying to get up to the top of his head. Another of his manias was a remarkable precision as to the time he took his meals, and he was so particular in this respect that he would lay his watch before him on the table at the hour of meal, and if the latter was not ready at the precise moment appointed, he would obstinately refuse to partake thereof.

On the thirtieth of June, 1846, Jackson graduated at West-Point, being the seventeenth in a class of fifty-nine, a class which was considered the most remarkable of any that ever graduated from that Academy. By a strange coïncidence there appear in the list of this class the names of many military officers who already have figured prominently, or at the present time hold important positions in both the Northern and Southern armies. Among these names we find those of McClellan, Stoneman, Foster, Sturges, Couch, Reno, Seymour, and many others equally or less distinguished.

Immediately after young Jackson had graduated at West-Point, he entered the army of the United States as a Brevet

Second Lieutenant of the First artillery, and received his full commission on the succeeding third of March. Among the officers of the First artillery at this period were the following military men who either have taken, or at the present time are taking prominent parts in the present war. On the side of the North, Justin Dimick, W. H. French, J. Hooker, L McDowell, J. B. Ricketts, J. M. Brannan, Seth Williams, Abner Doubleday, E. C. Boynton, T. Seymour, and others; and on the side of the South, J. H. Winder, J. B. Magruder, J. W. Mackall, A. P. Hill, and others.

At the commencement of the campaign in Mexico, Jackson proceeded to that country, as one of the officers of Magruder's battery. He took part in all the battles of that campaign, and was several times rewarded with promotion for his gallant and meritorious conduct therein. For the bravery which he displayed in the battles of Contreras and Cherubusco he was raised to the rank of Lieutenant on August twentieth, 1847, with the additional brevet rank of Captain, which bore the same date, but which was not awarded until August of the following year. He so much further distinguished himself at the battle of Chepultepec on the thirteenth of September, 1847, that in March, 1849, he received the brevet rank of Major—the commission for which was dated from the day on which the action took place. The *Army Register* and the actual history and facts of the Mexican war do not furnish the name of another person entering that war without position or office who attained the high rank of Major in the brief campaign and series of battles from Vera Cruz to the City of Mexico.

Several instances are recorded of the gallantry which was displayed by Jackson at the battle of Chepultepec. Magruder being a man of remarkably intemperate habits, it almost invariably happened that during the Mexican campaign, the chief command of his battery devolved on Lieutenant Jackson. Upon the eve of this battle Jackson, who then had charge of the battery, was advancing with it toward the scene of the following day's engagement, when, on turning a bend of the road, he found his progress arrested by a battery of four guns which the Mexicans had planted behind a small earth-work. A fight ensued, in which every horse and man in Jackson's command were killed or wounded, he only being left unharmed. The Mexicans rushed upon the battery, but the young officer would not leave his guns, when fortunately his enemies were suddenly outflanked, and compelled to retire in great haste, leaving him in indisputable possession thereof.

It is also related that at the battle of Chepultepec, Jackson was ordered by Pillow, to whose division Magruder's battery was attached, to withdraw his section, as his superior officer considered that it was too much exposed. He gave no heed, however, to the General's order, but rapidly limbered up, and moved his guns a hundred yards nearer the enemy's works, on which he did great execution.

Another anecdote related of Jackson's behavior in this engagement states that, upon the Fourteenth regular infantry being ordered to charge up a road, the men seemed dis-inclined to advance, in consequence of the heavy fire to which they were exposed. Jackson, upon perceiving this, stepped forward amid a shower of missiles and exclaimed, "You see, my men, there is no danger, follow me!" which daring act so inspired the troops that they immediately sprang forward to the charge.

The gallantry displayed by the young soldier throughout the entire of the battle of Chepultepec was of such a nature as to gain for him special mention in the official despatches of the Commander-in-Chief; an honor which was not award-ed to any other officer. In these despatches General Scott alluded to him as "the brave Lieutenant Jackson."

The career of a soldier in time of peace is so generally un-interesting and so unmarked by important events, that it is barren of interest to the public. The proceedings of to-day are almost a repetition of those of yesterday, and with the exception of the time occupied in the removal from fort to fort, the story of a day is but an epitome of a soldier's life at such a time. For the three or four years that succeeded the Mexican war, Jackson's life was no exception to this general rule.

On February twenty-ninth, 1852, Jackson retired from the army of the United States, having served therein nearly six years. After his retirement he took up his residence in his native State of Virginia, and became a Professor of Mathe-matics in the Military College of Lexington in that State.

Although he had a very fine class of pupils, his services at this establishment were not very conspicuous. Colonel Gilham was considered as the military genius of the school, and Jackson was but little thought of by the small hero-worshippers of Lexington. He was devoutly religious in all his actions, and stern in the performance of his duties; and, as is too often the case with such professors, he was not viewed with much favoritism by his pupils.

During the period of his professorship Jackson had a narrow escape from assassination, the consummation of which he averted by his great coolness and fearlessness of death. The person by whom his life was threatened was a cadet who had been dismissed from the institution. The youth actually went to the extremity of lying in wait for him on the road leading from the Institute to the village. As Jackson, in his accustomed walk toward the village, approached the spot where his enemy awaited him, a bystander called out to him of his danger. "Let the assassin murder if he will," replied the Professor, as he walked in the most unconcerned manner toward the young man, who slunk abashed from his path.

Perhaps none of the acquaintances of Jackson were more surprised at his brilliant exhibition of genius in this war, than were those who knew his blank life at the Institute, and were familiar with the stiff and uninteresting figure that was to be seen every Sunday in a pew of the Presbyterian church at Lexington. But true genius awaits occasion commensurate with its power and aspiration. The spirit of Jackson was trained in another school than that of West-Point or Lexington, and had it been confined there it never would have illuminated the page of history. How peculiarly appropriate, in such a case, would these oft-quoted lines of Gray's Elegy have applied to him :

> "Full many a gem, of purest ray serene,
>    The dark, unfathomed caves of ocean bear;
> Full many a flower is born to blush unseen,
>    And waste its sweetness on the desert air."

During the time of Jackson's residence in Lexington, he became connected with the Presbyterian church of that place. Of this denomination he was an earnest member, and, in fact, throughout his future life he displayed those eminently religious qualities which so elevate man in the estimation of his fellow-beings, but which are so rarely found in the camp or on the battle-field. He held the position of a deacon in the church to which he belonged, and participated in the councils thereof.

Whilst residing in Lexington, he became acquainted with the family of the Rev. George Junkin, D.D., whose daughter he married in the year 1853. But, unfortunately, in the following year, the occurrence of an event which usually adds to the happiness of a married life was to him a source of sorrow, and deprived him not only of his wife, but of the infant offspring she had borne him.

Jackson was married a second time in the year 1857 to a daughter of the Rev. Dr. Morrison, a Presbyterian minister, and President of Davidson College, North-Carolina, by whom he had one child, who was about six months old at the time of its father's death. This second wife is related to General D. H. Hill of the Confederate army.

# CHAPTER II.

## THE UPPER POTOMAC.

Jackson resigns his Professorship and joins the Confederate Army—Becomes a Colonel—Joins Johnston's Forces on the Upper Potomac—Rebel Evacuation of Harper's Ferry—Scenes of Devastation—Encounter with Patterson at Falling Waters—Jackson's First Display of Strategetic Ability—Johnston eludes Patterson and joins Beauregard—Jackson made a Brigadier-General.

AT the commencement of the Rebellion, Jackson was busily engaged with his professional duties at Lexington, and it was not until the secession of his State that he resigned his peaceful occupation for the hazards and excitements of a soldier's life. Like his celebrated companion in arms, General Lee, he was a theoretical Unionist up to the very date of Virginia's secession, struggling long in deciding between his duty to his country and his devotion to his State; and it was only when his own State drew the sword that he determined to follow her fortunes. This occurred at the latter end of April, 1861. His first command was a regiment of infantry, which he drilled so quickly, and yet so perfectly, that he was enabled to rely upon it at any moment. He was commissioned Colonel by the Governor of Virginia, and was with his regiment attached to the forces of General Johnston on the Upper Potomac.

2

It will be remembered that on the nineteenth of April, shortly after the commencement of the Rebellion, the Federals evacuated Harper's Ferry, after partially destroying the public works and armory there situated. Around this place—which is of historic interest from its having been the scene of that insurrection, small in itself but great in the influences it created, which in 1859 caused the name of John Brown to become celebrated in song and renowned in story—nature has lavished a wild beauty. On every side are seen the lofty ridges of the Blue Mountains, pierced at one bold point by the Potomac and the Shenandoah, whilst the railroad which here crosses the former stream, acts as a connecting-link between this bold mountain scenery and the great cities of the East and the West. It was in the neighborhood of these scenes that Jackson gathered the first leaves of that laurel-wreath with which his memory is now crowned.

The demonstrations of the Federal army in the Valley of Virginia were of such a nature that it was considered necessary to thwart them by the falling back of the Confederate army from Harper's Ferry to Winchester. General Patterson's approach was expected by the great route into the Valley from Pennsylvania and Maryland, leading through Winchester; and it was an object of the utmost importance to the Confederates that they should prevent any junction between his forces and those of General McClellan, who was already making his way from Western Virginia to the upper portions of the Valley. On the morning of the thirteenth of June, information was received from Winchester that Romney was occupied by two thousand Federal troops, supposed to be the vanguard of McClellan's army. A detachment was therefore despatched by railroad to check the Union advance; and on the morning of the fifteenth, the Confederate army left Harper's Ferry for Winchester.

The Rebels found it necessary the next morning to retire from their possession of the Ferry, and their destruction of the buildings, which had been left unscathed at the time of the evacuation of the place by the Federals, brought one of those wild, fearful scenes which make the desolation that grows out of war. This devastation is thus described: " The splendid railroad-bridge across the Potomac — one of the most superb structures of its kind on the continent — was set on fire at its northern end, while about four hundred feet at its southern extremity was blown up, to prevent the flames from reaching other works which it was necessary to save. Many of the vast buildings were consigned to the flames. Some of them were not only large but very lofty, and crowned with tall towers and spires, and we may be able to fancy the sublimity of the scene, when more than a dozen of these huge fabrics crowded into a small space were blazing at once. So great was the heat and smoke, that many of the troops were forced out of the town, and the necessary labors of the removal were performed with the greatest difficulty."

The Confederates received information on the day after their evacuation of Harper's Ferry, that General Patterson's army had crossed the Potomac at Williamsport; also that the Federal force at Romney had fallen back. The Rebels were therefore ordered to gain the Martinsburgh turnpike by a flank movement to Bunker's Hill, in order to place themselves between Winchester and the expected advance of Patterson. On learning this, the Federals immediately crossed the river. Resuming his first direction and plan, General Johnston proceeded to Winchester, so that his army might be in a position to oppose either General McClellan from the west, or Patterson from the north-east, and to form a junction with General Beauregard when necessary.

Intelligence having been received by the Confederates indicating a further movement by General Patterson, Colonel Jackson with a brigade was sent to the neighborhood of Martinsburgh to support Colonel Stuart, who had been placed in observation with his cavalry on the line of the Potomac. On the second of July, General Patterson crossed the river, and Colonel Jackson, pursuant to instructions, fell back before him, but in retiring, he engaged the Federal advance at Falling Waters, with a battalion of the Fifth Virginia regiment and Pendleton's battery of field-artillery. Skilfully taking a position where the smallness of his force was concealed, he engaged the Federals for a considerable time, inflicted a heavy loss, and retired when about to be outflanked, scarcely losing a man, but bringing off forty-five prisoners. In this engagement, which was after all merely a skirmish, Jackson exhibited his ready-witted strategy, and concealed from his opponents the knowledge that they were fighting an insignificant force, skilfully disposed to conceal their weakness, while Johnston was making his dispositions in the rear. The Confederate forces engaged in this action were four regiments of infantry and one regiment of cavalry, together with four pieces of artillery, mostly rifled.

The Northern reports inform us that between three and seven o'clock of the day in question, the Federal troops which had been concentrating at Hagerstown and Williamsport, Maryland, for several days previous, crossed the ford at the latter place. The morning was bright and beautiful, and the soldiers were in high spirits. The advancing force approached the enemy within a distance of seventy-five yards, and a brisk encounter ensued, without much loss on the Northern side. In anticipation of a retreat by the Federal forces, the Confederates had levelled the fences on both sides of the turnpike even with the ground, so as to cut them off in the event of their retiring to the Potomac. The first stand was made at Parkerfield farm, near Haynesville, where it was necessary to destroy a barn and other outbuildings, so that the Federals could make a charge upon the enemy. Here the conflict was fierce, the Rebels standing well up to their work, and finally, slowly retreating, knapsacks and canteens being hastily thrown aside as incumbrances to a backward march, and blankets and other articles of value left behind.

Upon receipt of the intelligence that Jackson had found it necessary to retire before the advancing forces of General Patterson, the Confederate force at Winchester, strengthened by recent arrivals, were ordered forward to his support. General Johnston took up a position within six miles of Martinsburgh, which town was now invested by the Federals, and for four days waited, with the expectation that he might be there attacked; but after being convinced that Patterson would not approach him, he returned to Winchester. General Johnston having placed Colonel Stuart to watch the Federal General's proceedings, he became enabled by the seventeenth of July to penetrate Patterson's design, and to ascertain that his object was to keep him in check, while General McDowell could attack the forces of Beauregard at Manassas. Our readers will readily recollect the obloquy which fell upon the name of General Patterson for his failure in the execution of that part of the military plan with which he was intrusted. Had he fulfilled his instructions, and prevented Johnston from uniting his forces to those of Beauregard, the story of the battle of Bull Run might perhaps have been told with a termination different to that which is now appended to it in the pages of history.

The marks of active determination which Colonel Jackson displayed and the military skill which he exhibited in the engagement at Falling Waters, and in the short campaign on the Upper Potomac, obtained for him promotion to the position of Brigadier-General.

# CHAPTER III.

## THE BATTLE OF BULL RUN.

Jackson's Position at the Opening of the Battle — His Timely Appearance upon the Principal Scene—Origin of the Sobriquet "Stonewall"—Description of the Main Battle-Ground — Desperate Position of the Confederates — Terrible Conflicts between the Opposing Forces — Gallantry of Jackson's Brigade — The Federals finally Repulsed — They become Panic-Stricken — Reasons why they were not Pursued by the Rebels — Beauregard's Official Remarks on Jackson's Heroism — His Appearance on the Field of Battle.

THE affair at Falling Waters was, after all, but the prologue to the great military drama in which the subject of our memoir was to play so important a part. The scene of the first great act was the battle-field of Bull Run, or Manassas, as it is termed by the people of the South. At this battle Jackson had the command of the First Virginia brigade, which consisted of five regiments, and the manner in which he handled this force, in several of the critical periods of the action, is considered by General Beauregard to have contributed largely to the Confederate success.

Jackson's brigade was amongst the first of the forces of General Johnston who, after they had eluded Patterson, hastened to the support of General Beauregard at Manassas.

At the opening of the engagement, shortly after dawn,

on July twenty-first, Jackson was placed as a support to General Bonham, who was detailed to guard Mitchell's Ford. About half-past seven o'clock A.M., his brigade was deployed along with Imboden's, and five pieces of Walton's battery, to take up a position along Bull Run. In the heat of the forenoon's engagement, when the Confederate forces were driven back, and the goddess of victory for the time seemed to smile upon the Union arms, the brigade under General Jackson got separated from Imboden's and Walton's commands; but being afterward reünited, they took up another position below the brim of the plateau, nearly east of the Henry House, and to the left of a ravine and woods occupied by the mingled remnants of other commands. It was here that the battle was to rage so long and so furiously, and where for some time the Rebels had to fight desperately against fearful odds, so that they could hold their own until their reënforcements could reach them.

Jackson's timely arrival at this point, as we shall hereafter show, was considered by General Beauregard to have contributed greatly to the change in the fortune of war, which was shortly to be experienced by the Confederates. It also gave to his troops an opportunity of winning for themselves a renown and an imperishable name. Jackson felt every confidence in the prowess of his force, and the reply which, upon this field, he made to his Commanding General, obtained for him that sobriquet which history will ever connect with his name. Beauregard fancying that his troops were raw, asked Jackson if he thought that they would be likely to stand. "Yes," replied he, "like a stone wall." But Jackson, with his usual modesty, ever after insisted that the name which has now become a type of valor belonged properly to the brigade which he commanded and not to its commander.

The topographical features of the plateau, now the stage of the contending armies, is thus described by General Beauregard, in his Report of the day's proceedings. "A glance at the map will show that it is inclosed on three sides by small water-courses, which empty into Bull Run within a few yards of each other, half a mile to the south of the Stone Bridge. Rising to an elevation of quite one hundred feet above the level of Bull Run at the bridge, it falls off on three sides to the level of the inclosing streams in gentle slopes, but which are furrowed by ravines of irregular direction and length, and studded with clumps and patches of young pines and oaks. The general direction of the crest of the plateau is oblique to the course of Bull Run in that quarter, and on the Brentsville and turnpike roads which intersect each other at right angles. Completely surrounding the two houses before mentioned, (as being situated upon this plateau,) are small open fields of irregular outline, and exceeding one hundred and fifty acres in extent. The houses occupied at the time — the one by Widow Henry, and the other by the free negro Robinson — are small wooden buildings, densely embowered in trees, and environed by a double row of fences on two sides. Around the eastern and southern brim of the plateau, an almost

3*

unbroken fringe of second growth pines gave excellent shelter for our marksmen, who availed themselves of it with the most satisfactory skill. To the west, adjoining the fields, a broad belt of oaks extends directly across the crest on both sides of the Sudley Road, in which, during the battle, regiments of both armies met and contended for the mastery. From the open ground of this plateau, the view embraces a wide expanse of woods and gently undulating, open country of broad grass and grain-fields in all directions."

Such are the general features and the surroundings of the spot for the possession of which, during this eventful day, the contending forces of the Federals and the Confederates disputed with varying success. Though the clangor of arms, the roll of musketry, and the roar of cannon indicated that the battle was raging far and wide, yet it was upon this stage that were enacted the most eventful scenes of the contest, and as it was principally in these scenes that General Jackson played his part in the drama of the day, they naturally form the only ones which come within the scope of our work.

This plateau was, during the morning, occupied by a division of the Confederate army under General Bee, but shortly after mid-day it was dislodged therefrom by the Federals. Overwhelmed by the surging mass of Northern troops, which pressed heavily upon the Rebels, the lines of the latter fell back. As the shattered battalions retired, the slaughter was terrible. They fell back in the direction of the Robinson

House, and were compelled to engage the Federals at several points in their retreat, losing both officers and men, in
order to keep them from closing in around them. It was at
this period of the battle that the telegraphic wires flashed
the news of victory to the people of the North—news which
was, alas, too soon to be followed by sinister intelligence of
a defeat at once complete and disastrous.

The retreat of the Confederates was finally arrested, just
in rear of the Robinson House, by the energy and resolution
of General Bee, assisted by the support of the Hampton Le-
gion and the timely arrival of Jackson's brigade of five regiments. A moment before, General Bee had been well-nigh
overwhelmed by superior numbers. He approached General
Jackson with the pathetic exclamation, " General, they are
beating us back;" to which the latter promptly replied:
" Sir, we'll give them the bayonet." General Bee immediately rallied his overtasked troops with the words : " There
is Jackson standing like a stone wall. Let us determine to
die here, and we will conquer."

The intentions of the Federals now became developed in
the minds of the Commanding Generals, and they were enabled to discern that the conflict which was raging in the
vicinity of Mitchell's Ford was merely a feint, and that the
triumph of the day would have to be decided upon or around
the plateau which has been described. Generals Johnston and Beauregard were four miles distant from this
critical scene of action, having placed themselves upon a
commanding hill to observe the movements. There could

be no mistake now of the Federal intentions, from the violent firing on the left and the immense clouds of dust raised by the march of a large body of troops from their centre.

At this important moment General Beauregard received information that certain instructions, which he had forwarded relative to an attack upon the Federal flank and rear at Centreville, had miscarried. It therefore now became necessary to depend on new combinations, and to meet the National forces upon the field on which they had chosen to give battle. It was plain that nothing but the most rapid combinations, and the most heroic and devoted courage on the part of the Rebel troops, could retrieve the field, which, according to all military conditions, appeared to be positively lost.

About noon, the scene of the battle is described as being utterly sublime. Not until then could one of the present generation, who had never witnessed a grand battle, have imagined such a spectacle. The hill occupied in the morning by Generals Beauregard and Johnston and their respective staffs placed the whole scene before one—a grand, moving diorama. When the firing was at its height, the roar of artillery reached the hill like that of protracted thunder. For one long mile, the whole valley was a boiling crater of dust and smoke. In the distance rose the Blue Ridge, to form the dark background of a most magnificent picture.

The condition of the battle-field was now at least desperate for the Confederates, and their left flank being now over-powered, it became necessary to bring immediately up to their support the reserves not already in motion. Dashing on at headlong gallop, Generals Johnston and Beauregard reached the field of action not a moment too soon. They were instantly occupied with the reörganization of the troops, and the presence of the two commanders upon the field and under fire, had a most salutary effect upon the men, and order was soon restored. To reöccupy the pla-teau was now the object of the Confederates, and for this purpose they planted their artillery upon an open space of limited extent, behind a low undulation, just at the eastern verge of the plateau, some five hundred or six hundred yards from the Henry House, and upon a level with that held by the batteries of the National army. From the action of these guns, and from the galling fire of musketry placed under cover upon the right and left flank, the Fed-eral force suffered so dreadfully that, according to the re-ports of its generals, regiment after regiment, which was thrown forward to dislodge the Rebels, was broken, never to recover its entire organization on that field.

In the mean time also two companies of Stuart's Rebel cavalry made a dashing charge down the Brentsville and Sudley road upon the New-York Fire Zouaves — then the Federal right on the plateau — which added to the disorder which the Confederate musketry wrought on their flank. However, the Union forces still pressed the Rebels heavily in that quarter of the field, and threw out fresh troops to

8

outflank them. Some three guns of a battery belonging to the former, in an attempt to obtain here a position apparently to enfilade the batteries of the latter, were thrown so close to a regiment of Jackson's brigade that the soldiers sprang forward and seized them with severe loss, but they were subsequently driven back by an overpowering force of Federal musketry.

At two o'clock in the afternoon, General Beauregard gave orders for the right of his line, except his reserves, to advance to recover the plateau. It was done with uncommon resolution and vigor. At the same time Jackson's brigade pierced the Federal centre with the determination of veterans, but it suffered seriously. With equal spirit the other parts of the Rebel line made the onset, and the Federal lines were broken and swept back at all points from the open ground of the plateau. The latter, however, soon strongly reënforced by fresh regiments, re-commenced the conflict, pressed the Confederate lines back, recovered their ground, and renewed the offensive.

Between half-past two and three o'clock P.M., the Confederates were also strongly reënforced by troops pushed forward from the rear by General Johnston, who had about noon repaired thither for the purpose of despatching the reserves to those positions on the field of battle where they were most required. General Beauregard received these reënforcements just as he had ordered forward to a second effort, for the recovery of the disputed plateau, the whole line, including his reserves. At this crisis of the battle, he felt called upon to lead in person. The attack was general, and was shared in by every Rebel regiment then on the field. The Confederates again swept the whole ground clear of the Union forces, and the plateau around the Henry and Robinson houses remained finally in their possession. But this victory was purchased with the lives of General Bee, Colonel Bartow, and many officers of distinction in the Confederate army.

The Rebels now, rapidly receiving the reënforcements which had been despatched from the rear under the direction of General Johnston, and which included troops that had only arrived at noon by railroad from the Valley of the Shenandoah, commenced to dislodge the Federals from the adjoining woods, in which they swarmed. Having accomplished this task, they commenced the pursuit of the Union army, which had become panic-stricken, and was in retreat. Being encumbered with prisoners which they had captured, a portion of the Confederate forces were compelled to desist from the pursuit, whilst the brigades of Generals Bonham and Longstreet followed the flying army nearly as far as Centreville, until night and darkness came on, when they retired from farther pursuit and returned to Bull Run.

General Beauregard admits that his troops were so exhausted from the laborious operations of the day—operations which had to be performed under cover of a burning July sun, and without water and without food, except a meal hastily snatched at dawn—that a general pursuit upon that evening was physically impossible; whilst on the following day an unusually heavy and unintermitting fall of rain intervened to obstruct his advance with reasonable prospect of fruitful results. Added to this, he states that the want of a cavalry force of sufficient numbers, made an efficient pursuit a military impossibility.

Among the panegyrics which the Confederate Commander passed upon the various officers of his army who specially distinguished themselves upon this eventful day, General Jackson's conduct, he stated to have been that of "an able, fearless soldier and sagacious commander, one fit to lead his brigade." He further said that "his efficient, prompt, timely arrival before the plateau of the Henry House, contributed much to the success of the day. Although painfully wounded in the hand, he remained on the field to the end of the battle, rendering invaluable assistance."

With regard to Jackson's personal appearance at the battle of Manassas, a Southern newspaper contained at the time some paragraphs which expressed great merriment at the first apparition of the future hero on the battle-field. His queer figure on horseback, and his habit of settling his chin in his stock, were also very amusing to some correspondents, who made flippant jests thereat in some of the Southern newspapers. These jests were, however, soon forgotten and forgiven in the tributes of admiration and love which afterward ensued to the popular hero of the war.

# CHAPTER IV.

## WINTER CAMPAIGN ON THE UPPER POTOMAC.

Lull in Military Proceedings — Jackson placed in Command on the Upper Potomac—March to Hancock—Severity of the Weather and Suffering of the Troops—Skirmish at Bath—Engagement at Hancock—Results of the Expedition—Jackson's Energy as a Commander—His Endurance of Fatigue—Illustrations of his Piety.

Both the Federal and Confederate armies that held joint possession of the sacred soil of Virginia, were so prostrated by the extraordinary exertions which they had made during the day upon which was fought the memorable battle of Bull Run, that for many months to come, they felt little inclined to renew active operations.

The Northern army, now placed under the charge of General McClellan, had little other occupation than the daily drill, and for a lengthened period the telegraphic wires flashed from its camp scarcely any intelligence of its proceedings beyond the well-worn and stereotyped phrase of "All quiet on the Potomac." If the military schoolmasters in the Federal army now busied themselves in teaching "the young idea how to shoot," the Confederate preceptors were not the less active in imparting the necessary rules of military science. General Jackson took advantage of this period of abstinence from active operations to raise both officers and men under his command to a state of military discipline which their future actions proved to have been of the highest order.

The energy and abilities displayed by General Jackson at the battle of Bull Run, were sufficiently prominent to mark him out for a separate command. Consequently, during the closing days of 1861, he was despatched with a force of about ten thousand men, from General Johnston's line, to Winchester, for the purpose of watching and impeding the progress of a portion of the Federal army, who were then in possession of the Upper Potomac, and who threatened the Valley of the Shenandoah. It has been considered by a Southern writer, that had the same force been placed at his command in early autumn, "with the view to an expedition to Wheeling, by way of the Winchester and Parkersburgh road, the good effects would, in all probability, have shown themselves in the expulsion of the Federals from North-Western Virginia." Though the people of the North may dispute the accuracy of these presumptions, it is needless at this date to cavil thereat.

At the commencement of 1862, portions of several Federal regiments were quartered at Hancock, a small town on a bend of the Upper Potomac, at Bath, a village in Virginia, some six miles south of that place, and at other points contiguous to these two places. General Jackson was desirous of dislodging the Union troops from these positions, which they evidently intended to hold throughout the remainder of the winter. For this purpose, therefore, on the first of January, 1862, his command left Winchester and proceeded on the road toward Romney, a small town to the north-west of that place, when it filed to the right, and marched toward Morgan County. Though the weather on the first day of the march was pleasant, the second was remarkably cold, and the road to be traversed was so bad, that the wagons could not keep up with the troops, which necessitated the men to lie out upon the ground, without covering, and to suffer from the want of food. The wagons, however, came up on the following morning, and the troops, after partaking of breakfast, proceeded on their march, but continued to suffer from the severity of the weather.

Another night was passed but with little rest; after which they proceeded on their journey, their sufferings being augmented by an increase in the coldness, to which was added a heavy snow-storm. When within four miles of the town of Bath, they met and drove back a small Federal force. Shortly after this the Confederates encamped for the night, but it was such a night that few except those accustomed to the hardships of a soldier's life when on active service, have ever the misfortune to experience. Though snow, rain, and hail alternately fell the whole night upon the prostrate troops, who were compelled to endure the same without blankets or covering of any kind, they were so completely exhausted that they fell down before the blazing fires which they had kindled, and slept soundly upon the wet ground. Approaching Bath, on the following morning, they announced their arrival by a discharge of cannon upon that place, in which several Union troops had taken up their winter quarters. The Federals replied to this volley from two batteries, but on some of the Rebel troops being deployed to charge these batteries, the soldiers spiked their guns, and rapidly fell back to the banks of the Potomac, hotly pursued by Ashby's cavalry, followed by infantry and artillery. The Federals having reached the river-bank before the arrival of the Rebel cavalry, they placed themselves in ambush, and fired upon their pursuers, several of whom they seriously wounded. The latter then fell back upon the main body, who brought up their artillery and shelled the woods.

Leaving a picket-guard, the Confederate forces retired to the rear, and encamped for the night. The intensity of the cold had increased so much that the soles of the troops on duty froze to the ground, and their sufferings were truly terrible. On Sunday morning, January fifth, the Confederates advanced to the shores of the Potomac, from which they had been encamped only half a mile distant, and found themselves in front of the pretty little town of Hancock, which was situated upon the Maryland side of the river. In this place the Federals were quartered in considerable force. Upon his arrival, General Jackson sent a flag of truce, by Colonel Ashby, to the authorities of the town, notifying the inhabitants that they should vacate the place, as he intended to bombard it, and he gave them two hours to do so. In accordance with this demand,

General Lander, who was in command of the town, at once removed all the non-combatants therefrom. At the expiration of the time, the Confederate batteries, which had been previously placed in position, opened fire, and the Federals replied thereto, but their shots fell short. The bombardment continued for about an hour, after which time the firing on both sides ceased for the day, little or no damage having been suffered by either party. As General Jackson desired to avoid burning the town, no shells were discharged for that purpose.

On the following (Monday) morning, the Federals re-opened fire, their balls falling thickly among the Confederates, but doing little or no damage. The Rebels did not reply to this firing, but occupied themselves in carrying off army stores, clothing, and other property from the Commissary Department of the Federals, which was placed on the Virginia side of the Potomac. While this was in progress a detachment of the Confederates was deployed to make a detour for the purpose of burning the Capon bridge, and tearing up the rails of the Baltimore and Ohio Railroad. On their progress, however, they met and routed some Northern troops who were placed in ambush, after which they proceeded in their work of destruction, in which they were somewhat impeded by the long-range guns of their antagonists.

This expedition to the banks of the Upper Potomac resulted in the capture of several prisoners, the expulsion of the Federals from this part of Virginia, the destruction of a fine railroad bridge, and the possession of guns, clothing, and several wagon-loads of military stores. In it, however, the Rebels suffered less from the bullets of their foes than they did from the inclemency of the weather; and many a stout heart had to succumb to the terrible sufferings caused by exposure and exhaustion in the severest portion of the winter. Of General Jackson's conduct therein, it is stated that the heroic commander, whose courage had been so brilliantly illustrated at Manassas, gave new proofs of his iron will in this expedition, and in the subsequent events of his campaign in the upper portion of the Valley of Virginia. No one would have supposed that a man who, at the opening of the war, had been but a Professor in a State Military Institute, would have shown such active determination and such grim energy in the field.

To Jackson's merit as a commander, writes Mr. Edward A. Pollard, in his History of the first year of the War, "he added the virtues of an active, humble, consistent Christian, restraining profanity in his camp, welcoming army colporteurs, distributing tracts, and anxious to have every regiment in his army supplied with a chaplain. He was vulgarly sneered at as a fatalist; his habits of soliloquy were derided as superstitious conversations with a familiar spirit; but the confidence which he had in his destiny was the unfailing mark of genius, and adorned the Christian faith which made him believe that he had a distinct mission of duty in which he should be spared for the ends of Providence."

Of the habits of his life, the following description is

also given by one who knew him well: "He is as calm in the midst of a hurricane of bullets as he was in the pew of his church at Lexington, when he was Professor of the Institute. He appears to be a man of almost superhuman endurance. Neither heat nor cold makes the slightest impression upon him. He cares nothing for good quarters and dainty fare. Wrapped in his blanket, he throws himself down on the ground anywhere, and sleeps as soundly as though he were in a palace. He lives as the soldiers live, and endures all the fatigue and all the suffering that they endure. His vigilance is something marvellous. He never seems to sleep, and lets nothing pass without his personal scrutiny. He can neither be caught napping nor whipped when he is wide awake. The rapidity of his marches is something portentous. He is heard of by the enemy at one point, and before they can make up their minds to follow him he is off at another. His men have little baggage, and he moves as nearly as he can without incumbrance. He keeps so constantly in motion that he never has a sick-list, and no need of hospitals."

Among the many anecdotes which are current of General Jackson's mode of life, there is one which illustrates the earnestness of his piety, and his never-failing appeal to his Maker to view with favor his every undertaking. He had in his service a negro, who had become so accustomed to his ways that he was enabled to discern whenever he was about to start upon an expedition, without receiving any notice to that effect. When once asked how he was able to ascertain this, as his master never divulged his plans, the negro replied : "Massa Jackson allers prays ebery night and ebery mornin' ; but when he go on any expedishun, he pray two, or tree, or four times durin' de night. When I see him pray two, or tree, or four times durin' de night, I pack de baggage, for I know he gwine on an expedishun."

# CHAPTER V.

Jackson retires from the Upper Potomac—Skirmish at Blue's Gap—Encounter at Blooming Gap—Death of General Lander—Harper's Ferry reoccupied by the Federals—Advance of General Banks to Winchester—Skirmishes before the Battle—Country around Winchester—Opening of the Engagement—Terrific Conflict near a Stone Wall—The Confederates finally repulsed—Numbers and Losses of the Combatants.

ALTHOUGH Gen. Jackson was enabled, without much difficulty, to drive the small Federal force, which was stationed on the Virginia side of the Upper Potomac, to the northern banks of that river, yet he soon discovered that the ground which he had gained was untenable. He therefore speedily commenced to retrace his steps to the Valley of the Shenandoah, closely followed by the Federals under command of General Lander. On the morning of the seventh of January, 1862, a small force of Rebels, under the leadership of Colonel Blue, who had intrenched themselves at Blue's Gap —a pass strongly fortified by nature, and situated between two hills, a few miles to the east of Romney—were driven therefrom by a party of Union soldiers under Colonel Dunning, with a loss to the former of two guns and several men. On the seventh of February, General Lander occupied

3

Romney, the Confederates having previously evacuated that place and retreated toward Winchester.

On the fourteenth, with four hundred cavalry, he drove from Blooming Gap a considerable force of Confederates, and pursued them for eight miles beyond the Gap on the road toward Winchester, and across the line which divided his department from that of General Banks. This work was only accomplished through the dashing behavior of General Lander, who had to rally his soldiers after they had become panic-stricken. It resulted in the capture of a great number of Rebel officers and men, and a large amount of commissariat stores. It was during this engagement that the popular writer, Lieutenant Fitz-James O'Brien, who was aid-de-camp to the Commanding General, received a bullet-wound in his breast which afterward resulted in his death; and a fortnight after the battle the country had to mourn the loss of General Lander, who died in his camp from congestion of the brain, superinduced by the debilitating effects from the wound he had received near Edward's Ferry, in his reconnoissance the day after the fall of Colonel Baker. He was one of the bravest and most energetic officers, and one who had given the highest promise of valuable service to the Union in this its time of greatest need.

The Rebels had likewise previous to this encounter been routed at New-Creek, forty-five miles south of Romney, by another portion of General Lander's command, under Colonel Dunning. They were now completely driven out of the former's department.

In a previous chapter we have stated that Harper's Ferry, which was evacuated by the Federals at the beginning of the Rebellion, again fell into their hands upon the advance of General Patterson, when just before the battle of Bull Run, that officer was required to prevent a junction between the forces under the command of General Johnston, and those then situated at Manassas. This important position was afterward reöccupied by the Confederates, and was in their possession upon the second appearance of General Jackson in the region of the Upper Potomac. After that General was driven back by General Lander to the Valley of the Shenandoah, it was again deserted by the Rebels, and reöccupied by the National forces on February twenty-fourth. The place was, however, the scene of stirring events about three weeks previous to this date, when the greater part of what was left of it was reduced to ashes by the Federals, as a punishment to the Confederates for their having fired upon a boat of the former, which was sent to meet one of the latter, carrying a flag of truce.

Entering Virginia at the mouth of the Shenandoah, General Banks now commenced to pursue Jackson in his retrograde movement up the valley of that river, and on the last day of February occupied Charlestown, situated eight miles south of the Potomac, upon the line of railroad leading toward Winchester; and on March third he also took unopposed possession of Martinsburgh, on the Baltimore and Ohio Railroad, a few miles west of Harper's Ferry.

By a rearrangement of the Army of the Potomac, the same was now divided into five army corps, the fifth of which included the forces under General Shields, who had succeeded to the command of General Lander, and those of General Banks, the entire force to be under the command of the latter General.

Advancing in the wake of the retreating forces of General Jackson, the Union troops approached Winchester, and, after two skirmishes on the way, entered that town on the twelfth, a strong fort to the north of it having been evacuated by the Rebels on the previous evening. Here they were received with joyful acclamations, the people hailing the coming of the Union army as the harbinger of peace and future prosperity, and cheering the regiments as they passed, which cheers were warmly responded to by both officers and men. On the following afternoon, while a party of Union cavalry were foraging on the Strasburgh road, three miles from Winchester, and while the teams were being loaded with hay, they encountered a small force of Ashby's cavalry, with whom a skirmish took place, the latter advancing as the former returned to Winchester with their loaded teams, in good order and unharmed. General Banks on this day issued an order to his troops, in which he forbade depredations of any kind whatsoever, and deeply regretted that officers, in some cases, from mistaken views, had either tolerated or had encouraged such a course.

The people of the North will well remember how, at this time, like to a will-o'-the-wisp, Jackson retreated before the advancing Federals, being driven away in an inglorious retreat, and compelled to abandon the strongholds which he had held for six months. He, however, transported his baggage previous to the removal of his forces, which proves that the retreat had been carefully provided for. On the eighteenth and nineteenth of April, General Shields made a reconnoissance in the direction of Mount Jackson, a place situated on the Shenandoah River, at the termination of the Manassas Gap railroad. He there ascertained that the Confederates under Jackson were strongly posted near that place, and in communication with a large force at Luray and Washington to the east thereof. He deemed it important to draw Jackson from his position and supporting force if possible. To effect this, he fell back upon Winchester on the twentieth, giving his movement all the appearance of a hasty retreat. But, as it was scarcely considered likely that Jackson would fall into the trap laid for him, and as it was advisable that the army on the Rappahannock should be reënforced from Banks's *corps d'armee*, the first division of the latter was being removed upon the turnpike which leads directly from Winchester to Alexandria, and the last brigade left for Centreville, by the way of Berryville, on the morning of the twenty-second. Only Shields's division and the Michigan cavalry were now at Winchester.

The Confederate scouts, observing this movement, signalled Jackson, with fires upon the hill-tops, that Winchester was being evacuated by the Federal forces, and about five

o'clock P.M., some of Ashby's cavalry drove in the pickets
of the latter. The troops immediately sprung to their arms,
and two regiments of infantry, accompanied by two batteries of artillery, pushed forward and drove back the Confederates, who retreated, after a short resistance, to a little
distance beyond Kernstown, a small village on the Valley
turnpike, about three and a half miles southernly from
Winchester. During this attack, General Shields, while
directing one of the batteries to its position, was struck by
a shell which burst near him, broke his arm above the
elbow, and for the time entirely paralyzed one side of his
body. No one around supposed that he was injured, for
the old hero gave no word or sign of having been wounded,
but continued to give his orders, through his staff-officers,
as coolly and deliberately as if nothing had happened, until
every thing had been arranged to his satisfaction. This
was the fourth time that the General had received wounds
which had endangered his life, the three previous ones
having been received during the campaign in Mexico.

The General, divining the attack of the enemy to be only
a ruse to make him show his strength, kept the rest of his
forces out of sight; and though prostrated by the injuries
he had received, set to work to make the requisite disposition of his troops for the ensuing day. These dispositions
being made, the General rested as well as his wounds would
permit.

A brief description is here necessary of the approaches to
Winchester, and of the field which the next day became the

scene of one of the most bloody and desperately fought bat·
tles of the war, and the only one in which General Jackson
experienced a severe reverse. Winchester is approached
from the south by three principal roads. These are the
Cedar Creek road on the west, the Valley Turnpike leading
to Strasburgh in the centre, and the Front Royal road on the
east. On the Valley Turnpike, about three and a half miles
from Winchester, is the little village of Kernstown, already
mentioned; about half a mile north of this village and west
of the Valley Turnpike is a ridge of high hills commanding
the approach by the Valley road and a part of the surrounding country.

This ridge was the key-point of the Federal position, and
on this Colonel Kimball, the senior officer in command of
the field, took his station. Along this ridge Lieut.-Colonel
Daum, Chief of Artillery, posted three of his batteries, keeping one battery in reserve some distance in the rear. Part
of the Federal infantry was posted on this ridge, within
supporting distance of the artillery, and sheltered by the
irregularities of the hills.

The main body of the Confederates was posted in order
of battle, about half a mile beyond Kernstown, their line
extending about two miles from the Cedar Creek road on
their left, to a ravine near the Front Royal road on their
right. They had so skilfully selected their ground, that
while it afforded facilities for manœuvring, they were completely masked by high and wooded grounds in front, and
so adroitly did they conceal themselves, that at eight o'clock

A.M., of the twenty-third, nothing was visible but the force which had been repulsed the evening previous.

Being unable, in consequence of his wound, to reconnoitre the point in person, General Shields despatched an officer to perform that duty, who returned about an hour after, reporting that there were no indications of any hostile force, except that of Ashby's cavalry. General Shields and General Banks, after consulting together, came to the conclusion that Jackson was nowhere in the vicinity, and, therefore, General Banks took his departure for Washington. Although the conclusion had been reached that Jackson was not before Winchester, yet General Shields, knowing the ever-vigilant foe he had to deal with, did not neglect a single precaution. About half-past ten o'clock A.M., a Confederate battery opened upon the Federals, which disclosed to the latter indications that a considerable force of the former was planted in the woods. In consequence of this discovery, a brigade was pushed forward, and placed in a position to oppose the advance of the right wing of the Rebels.

The action opened by a fire of artillery on both sides, but at too great a distance to be very effective. The advance was made by the Confederates, who pushed a few more guns to their right, supported by a considerable force of infantry and cavalry, with the apparent intention of enfilading the Federal position and turning Shields's left flank. An active body of skirmishers was immediately thrown forward by the latter to check the advance of the

Rebels. These skirmishers were supported by four pieces of artillery and a brigade of infantry, and this united force repulsed the Confederates at all points. The latter withdrew the greater part of their force on their right, and formed it into a reserve to support their left. They then added their original reserve, and two batteries to their main body, and under shelter of a hill on their left, on which they had posted other batteries, they advanced their formidable column, with the evident intention of turning the Federal right flank, or overwhelming it. The National batteries on the opposite hill were soon found insufficient to check or even retard the Rebels. A message was therefore sent to General Shields informing him of the state of the field. Not a moment was to be lost. "Throw forward all your disposable infantry, carry the enemy's batteries, turn his left flank, and hurl it back on the centre," were his orders, and Colonel Kimball executed them with rapidity and vigor. The movement was intrusted to Tyler's splendid brigade, and following their intrepid leader, they pressed forward with enthusiasm to the performance of this perilous duty. The skirmishers of the Confederates were as chaff before the wind. Steadily onward it went until within a few yards of a high stone wall, behind which Jackson's men were securely posted, when it was met by a fire so fierce and deadly that its ranks melted away like frost before the morning sun. They wavered but for a moment, then rushed forward to the desperate struggle. At this juncture, Colonel Tyler was strongly reënforced; and

3*

with a cheer and a yell from his men that rose high and loud above the roar of battle, he drove the Rebels from their shelter, and through the woods, with a fire as destructive as ever fell upon a retreating foe. The Rebels fought desperately, as their piles of dead attested, and to their chagrin and mortification, Jackson's " invincible stonewall brigade " and the accompanying brigades were obliged to fall back upon their reserve in disorder. Here they took up a new position, and attempted to retrieve the fortunes of the day. But again rained down upon them the same close and destructive fire. Again cheer upon cheer rang in their ears. But a few minutes did they stand against it, when they turned and fled in dismay, leaving their killed and wounded on the field. Night alone saved them from destruction. They retreated about five miles, and then took up a position for the night. The Federal troops now threw themselves on the field to rest, and to eat the first meal they had been able to partake of since the dawning of the day.

Although the battle had been won, still General Shields could not believe that Jackson would have hazarded a decisive engagement at such a distance from his main body without expecting reënforcements. So to be prepared for any contingency, he brought together all the troops within his reach, and sent an express for Williams's brigade, now twenty miles distant on its way to Centreville, to march all night, and join him in the morning. He also gave positive orders to the forces in the field to open fire upon the Rebels as soon as daylight would enable them to point their guns, and to pursue them without respite, and compel them to abandon their guns and baggage, or cut them to pieces.

It appears that General Shields had rightly divined Jackson's intentions, for on the morning of the day of battle a reënforcement of five thousand men from Luray reached Front Royal, on their way to join him. This reënforcement was being followed by another body of ten thousand from Sperryville, but recent rains having rendered the Shenandoah River impassable, they were compelled to fall back without effecting the proposed junction.

At daylight on the twenty-fourth, the Federal artillery again opened on the Rebels, but the latter entered upon their retreat in good order, considering what they had suffered. General Banks, hearing of the engagement on his way to Washington, halted at Harper's Ferry, and ordered back a part of Williams's division. He returned to Winchester, and after making a hasty visit to General Shields, assumed command of the forces in pursuit of the flying Rebels. The pursuit was kept up with vigor until the Federals reached Woodstock, where Jackson's retreat became fright, when it was abandoned, in consequence of the utter exhaustion of the troops.

The Federal loss in this engagement is stated to have been one hundred and three in killed, four hundred and forty-one wounded, and twenty-four missing. Of the Confederate loss we are not able to speak with accuracy. General Shields reports that two hundred and seventy were found dead on the battle-field, and that forty were buried by the inhabitants of the adjacent village. He computes, from a calculation made of the number of graves discovered on both sides of the Valley road, between Winchester and Strasburgh, added to these figures, that Jackson's loss in killed could not have been less than five hundred, and that his wounded must have been double that number. Jackson's official report would no doubt satisfy us upon this head, but as the Confederate government have studiously abstained from making the same public, there can be little reason to imagine otherwise than that his loss was a severe one. In fact there can be no denying that this battle of Winchester terminated most disastrously to him, though perhaps it was the only one which has not been more or less instrumental in adding considerably to his fame.

The Federal force engaged in this battle did not exceed seven thousand in infantry, cavalry, and artillery. General Shields calculates that Jackson must have been supported by a much larger number, whilst Confederate correspondents claim that their force was considerably outnumbered by that of the Federals.

Though the battle of Winchester pales into insignificance when it is compared with many of the other conflicts of the present war — conflicts in which twenty times the number of troops were engaged—yet it has been scarcely surpassed by any in the terrible earnestness of the combatants and in the fierceness of the combat. It was a battle in which many for the first time bathed their swords in blood, but they fought like veterans, and were led by commanders worthy of their valor. Although Jackson on this occasion suffered the mortification of defeat, it might have been that had he been opposed by a less practised and a less gallant general than he found the Federal commander to be, his well-known strategy would have won for him the honors of the day. At one time victory appeared to be almost within his grasp. Fighting behind a veritable stone wall, his renowned "Stonewall" brigade poured forth into the Federal ranks their deadly missiles with such unerring aim, that nothing, but the most dogged courage of the Northern men, could have enabled them to dislodge their enemy from his mural breastwork. So terrible was this part of the engagement that, during its progress, four times was the color-bearer of the Fifth Ohio Volunteers laid prostrate, after which the banner was borne forward to victory by the Lieutenant-Colonel of another regiment, who had caught it from the hands of a dying sergeant.

# CHAPTER VI.

Retreat of Jackson up the Valley—Federal Plans to capture him—Battle
of McDowell—Compels Banks to retreat—Battle of Front Royal—Alarm
of General Banks at Strasburgh—He commences a rapid Retreat—Disas-
ters by the Way—Exciting Scenes in Winchester—Second Battle of Winchester—Safe Arrival of the Federals in Maryland—Estimate of Losses.

AFTER the battle of Winchester, General Jackson retreated toward the uppper waters of the Shenandoah, closely followed by the forces under Generals Banks and Shields,
who, however, were never able to come up with their swift-
footed antagonist. During this pursuit, they were several
times impeded in their progress by, and had many encoun-
ters with, Ashby's cavalry, who acted as the rear-guard of
the Rebels. They disputed the passage of the Federals at
nearly every point, burning bridges, and throwing every
obstacle in their progress.

On the fourth of April, the Federal troops in this valley
were detached from the Army of the Potomac, in which they
formed a *corps d'armée*, and the district was created into a sep-
rate Department, under the command of General Banks. It
was at this time also that the troops situated upon the Rap-

pahannock were in like manner detached from General Mc-
Clellan's supreme command and placed under that of Mc-
Dowell. These new arrangements are considered by some
to have considerably interfered with General McClellan's
plan of operations upon the Peninsula, from which point he
was now menacing Richmond.

The Confederates were desirous of collecting all their available strength for the protection of their capital, and orders
were forwarded shortly after this time to General Jackson,
instructing him to rejoin his forces to those of General Johnston; but at the earnest remonstrance of the former General,
who considered that he could better defend Richmond on
the Shenandoah than upon the Chickahominy, he was allowed to remain on the banks of the former river.

To capture Jackson and his entire force was one of the
cherished plans of the Federals. While General Banks was
closely treading in his footsteps in his retreat up the valley,
a strong detachment of the army under General Fremont,
who was in command of the Mountain Department of
the Alleghanies, was deployed under Generals Milroy and
Schenck, to enter the Shenandoah Valley at Buffalo Gap,
west of Staunton, and there give Jackson a meeting. It was
anticipated that, being thus placed between two fires, it
would be barely possible the Rebel General could escape. How far the Federals were right in their calcula-
tions, the sequel will tell.

In the movements of General Milroy, having for their object the circumvention of the Rebels, he encountered a por-

tion of Jackson's force on April the twenty-first, within a few miles of Buffalo Gap, and had a skirmish with a small force of their cavalry. He then fell back to McDowell, on the Bull Pasture Mountain, where he encamped till May the eighth, on which date he was driven therefrom by a superior force of Confederates.

General Jackson, learning the advance of Milroy, sent a force to meet him from Valley Mills, six miles north of Staunton, with five days' rations and without tents or baggage, save blankets, under the command of General Ed. Johnson. Upon the next day, the advance-guard had a skirmish with the outposts of the Federals at the junction of Jennings's Gap and the Parkersburgh turnpike-road, twenty-one miles from Staunton. At the same time, General Jackson came up with an additional force, and after consultation with General Johnson, the latter proceeded along the road toward Shenandoah Mountain in pursuit of the Federals, closely followed by the force under General Jackson. Arriving at the mountain, they discovered that several Federal regiments, which had been encamped there, had hastily retreated, leaving their tents and stores behind them; and, ascending to the summit, they could see them proceeding upon the east side of Bull Pasture Mountain, about five miles in advance.

At sunrise on the morning of the eighth, the Confederates continued their line of march, and arriving at Bull Pasture Mountain they ascended to its summit, and discovered that Milroy had placed a battery on the road leading into Mc-

Dowell, and commanding a narrow gorge on the west side of the mountain, through which the road passes. It becoming late in the day before the Confederate Generals had completed their survey of the Federal position, they concluded to postpone offensive operations until the following morning. But about five o'clock they were attacked by the National forces, who were reënforced, and after a desperate fight of five hours' duration drove them from the field. During the engagement, General Johnson narrowly escaped being captured. He was rescued from a perilous position by the Richmond Zouaves, who, observing his danger, charged upon the Federals, and by this act disobeyed orders which General Jackson had given them to fall back, the latter at the time not being aware of his brother General's critical position.

The Rebels lost on this occasion about three hundred in killed, wounded, and missing, of which one third were either killed or mortally wounded. The Federal loss is stated to have been thirty killed and two hundred and sixteen wounded. The entire force of the latter in the engagement was two thousand and sixty-five men, and of the former two brigades of three regiments each.

It was quite dark before the engagement terminated, when the Federals at once prepared to fall back, and found it necessary to destroy a quantity of stores. The Confederates expected to renew the fight the following morning, but found that their foe had evacuated his camp, leaving behind him all his equipage, a large quantity of ammunition, a number of cases of Enfield rifles, and about one hundred head of cattle, mostly milch cows.

The Federals made their retreat good to Franklin, west of the Shenandoah Mountains, to which place they were closely followed by the Confederates. General Fremont also reached this place on May the thirteenth, having proceeded thither by forced marches, it being apprehended that an attack would be made by the Rebels upon the Union forces there situated.

General Jackson having compelled the retreat of the forces of General Fremont, who had been sent to oppose his progress, now turned round upon General Banks, and instead of being the pursued became the pursuer. The rapidity with which, from this change in the programme, the latter General was compelled to make good his retreat to the northern banks of the Potomac, exhibited a display of strategetical ability on his part which was only equalled by that still greater strategy which necessitated the retreat.

The suddenness with which this scene in the drama of the war was changed from a bright and glowing prospect to one enveloped in mist and darkness was a cause of great alarm to the people of the North, and led the President not only to call for aid from the militia of the loyal States, but to prevent General McDowell from marching with his forces from the Rappahannock to the assistance of General McClellan in his attack upon Richmond.

The most southerly point which General Banks reached

in the Valley of the Shenandoah was Harrisonburgh, where, on April the twenty-ninth, a National salute was fired and rejoicings took place in honor of recent Union victories.

Shortly after this date, finding that Jackson was pressing upon his front and that the place was becoming untenable, the Federal General retreated down the valley. One of the immediate causes which necessitated this retreat was the removal of General Shields's division, of two thousand men or more, from General Banks's corps. There is reason to believe that urgent, but useless, remonstrance was made by General Banks against this depletion of his force, and that a representation which he had made, that Jackson had been heavily reënforced, was met only by incredulity. The number of men left under General Banks's command was but about seven thousand, who were now pressed by three times that number under Generals Jackson and Ewell.

On the twenty-first of May some of Ashby's cavalry showed themselves in the neighborhood of Strasburgh, from which place they were driven by a small force of Federal cavalry. About this time a considerable portion of Jackson's forces were making a detour to Front Royal—a small village twelve miles east of Strasburgh, and situated on the eastern bank of the Shenandoah River, over which is here carried a large bridge of the Manassas Gap Railroad—and on the twenty-third surprised and captured almost the entire Federal force, which was encamped near that place. This latter consisted of about nine hundred men under the command of Colonel John R. Kenly. They were stationed at Front

Royal, for the purpose of protecting the place and the railroad and bridges between that town and Strasburgh against the local guerrilla parties who infested that locality. So small a force could never have been expected to defend themselves against much larger numbers, for Front Royal in itself is an indefensible position. Two mountain valleys debouch suddenly upon the town from the south, commanding it by almost inaccessible hills, and it is at the same time exposed to flank movements by other mountain valleys *via* Strasburgh on the west, and Chester Gap on the east. The only practicable defence of this town would seem to be by a force sufficiently strong to hold these mountain passes some miles in advance, and such a force General Banks had not at his disposal.

On the twenty-third of May it was discovered that the entire Confederate force was in movement down the valley of the Shenandoah between the Massanutten Mountain and the Blue Ridge, and in close proximity to the town; and their cavalry had captured a considerable number of the Federal pickets, before the alarm was given of their near approach. The little band found itself instantaneously compelled to choose between an immediate retreat or a contest with overwhelming numbers. They chose the latter. Driven at last from the camp and the town, they were compelled to retreat across the river. Again forming into line and placing their battery in position upon the opposite shore, they opened fire upon the Rebels, while the latter were fording the stream. They again found it necessary to retreat, and had only proceeded two miles upon the Winchester road, when they were overtaken by the Rebel cavalry. A fearful fight ensued, which ended in a complete destruction of the command, Colonel Kenly falling at the head of his column. A very small number only were enabled to escape, accomplishing the same through the friendly covering of the neighboring woods.

Very early on the following morning, the Confederates marched upon the road to Middletown, a place situated on the turnpike between Strasburgh and Winchester, and about eight miles north of the former place. At Middletown they came upon and attacked a part of General Banks's force as it was retreating along the road. Having cut the same in twain, a brigade of Ewell's division pursued the Strasburgh wing, capturing many prisoners, and demoralizing the rest of the troops, whilst the main body hurried swiftly down the valley after General Banks. Every few hundred yards, they passed one or more Federal wagons, upset, broken, or teamless, and full of baggage or military stores. Upon approaching Newtown, a few miles north of Middletown, the Rebels were for a while checked with artillery, after which the Federal rout and flight became precipitous and exciting beyond degree. The Federals made another stand in the neighborhood of Winchester, but after an engagement of short duration, they were compelled to give up the contest, and continue their retreat.

On the evening of the twenty-third, information was re-

ceived by General Banks at Strasburgh of the critical position in which Colonel Kenly was placed at Front Royal;
but as he viewed with distrust the extravagant statements
which he received of the Confederate strength, he only forwarded a regiment of infantry, a detachment of cavalry, and
a section of artillery to his assistance. He had, however,
scarcely despatched these reënforcements when information
reached him of the utter annihilation of Colonel Kenly's
troops. He therefore recalled them, and sent out numerous reconnoitring parties to ascertain, if possible, the
force, and the position and purpose of this sudden movement
of General Jackson. It was soon found that his pickets were in possession of every road leading from Front
Royal to Strasburgh, Middletown, Newtown, and Winchester, and rumors from every quarter represented him
in movement in rear of his pickets in the direction of the
Federal camp.

General Banks could not now doubt the extraordinary
force of the Confederates by which he was threatened, nor
could he believe otherwise but that they had a more extensive purpose than the capture of the " brave little band at
Front Royal." He at once divined that this purpose could
be nothing less than either the defeat of his own command
or its possible capture by the occupation of Winchester,
through which means the Rebels would be enabled to intercept his supplies and reënforcements, and cut him off from
all possibility of retreat. He also ascertained that he was
menaced by the divisions of Generals Jackson, Ewell, and

Johnson, numbering not less than twenty-five thousand men, under command of the first-named General.

Considering his position a very critical one, General Banks felt that the most expedient course for himself to adopt was to make a rapid movement on Winchester with a view to anticipate the occupation of that town by Jackson. He would thus place his command in communication with its original base of operations in the line of reënforcements by Harper's Ferry and Martinsburgh, and by this means secure a safe retreat in case of disaster.

Calling in all his outposts, he prepared to march at three o'clock on the morning of the twenty-fourth of May. Several hundred disabled men who had been left in his charge by Shields's division, were first put upon the march, and his wagon train was ordered forward to Winchester, under an escort of cavalry and infantry. General Hatch, with nearly the whole force of cavalry and six pieces of artillery, was charged with the protection of the rear of the column, and the destruction of army stores for which transportation was not provided. All the preparations being completed with incredible alacrity, the column was put in motion shortly after nine o'clock. It had not proceeded many miles when information was received from the front that the Rebels had attacked the train, and were in full possession of the road at Middletown. This report was soon confirmed by the return of fugitives, refugees, and wagons, which came tumbling to the rear in dreadful confusion. The immediate danger being now in front, the troops were ordered to the head of the column, and the train transferred to the rear. Cedar Creek Bridge, three miles north of Strasburgh,—over which the entire column had passed, with the exception of the rear-guard, which had been instructed to remain in front of Strasburgh as long as possible, and thus hold the enemy in check in that direction —was also prepared for the flames, in order that its destruction might prevent any pursuit on the part of the Confederates. By the burning of the bridge, Captain Abert and the *Zouaves d'Afrique* were cut off from the column, but after a sharp conflict with a party of Rebel cavalry at Strasburgh, they made their way safely to Williamsport, where they joined their comrades.

The advance-guard encountered the Confederates in force at Middletown, thirteen miles south of Winchester, and after a sharp engagement drove them back. The column had not, however, proceeded much farther, before it was again attacked by a considerable force of infantry, cavalry, and artillery. After repeated attempts to force a passage through the Rebel lines which had possession of the turnpike, a part of the force which had been cut off from the main body made several ineffectual attempts to join it by proceeding upon a parallel road. Failing in this, they returned to Strasburgh, from which place they proceeded by a circuitous route to Winchester, and other places north thereof, where they joined the main body.

The rear of the column was again attacked by an increased force between Newtown and Kernstown, and large bodies of Jackson's cavalry passed upon the Federal right and left, the increased vigor of his movements demonstrating the rapid advance of his main body.

The early and rapid march of the front portion of the train prevented the accomplishment of Jackson's contemplated plan of crushing it between those forces which he had despatched to intercept it, and the troops which pressed upon the rear of the column. It was, therefore, only the end of the column which encountered the main difficulties that beset it on its journey. Those of the front who, after a long and anxious day's march, were enabled to retire to rest in the town of Winchester on the evening of that eventful Saturday, were startled at daybreak on the Sabbath morning by the noise of cannon and the rattle of musketry, and could see the smoke as it rose from the hills three miles distant. Some of the people of Winchester gazed thitherward, as upon an interesting spectacle, and rejoiced that Jackson was again coming to free them from the Northern yoke; whilst others could see nothing in the anticipated change which could give them cause for joy.

Presently, and there were heard the tramping of horses' hoofs upon the road, and the heavy rolling of artillery over the pavement, and then every thing was in commotion. The women sobbed, and the men ran to and fro. The forces which had been quartered for the night in the town were started upon a hasty retreat. Flames rose from burning buildings, and heavy columns of smoke which roll-

4

ed upward, betokened to distant eyes that a scene of destruction was being enacted.

Whilst the Confederates were entering the town at the southern end, the Federals were rapidly making their exit through its northern portals. "All the streets were in commotion," writes an eye-witness to the scene; "Cavalry were rushing disorderly away, and infantry frightened by the rapidity of their mounted companions, were in consternation. All were trying to escape faster than their neighbors, dreading most of all to be the last. . . . . Guns, knapsacks, cartridge-boxes, bayonets, and bayonet-cases, lay scattered upon the ground in great profusion, thrown away by the panic-stricken soldiers. . . . . But this confusion and disorder was not of long duration. General Banks riding continually among the men, and addressing them kindly and firmly, shamed them to a consideration of their unbefitting consternation. At length stationing himself and staff with several others across a field through which the soldiers were rapidly flying, the men were ordered to stop their flight, were formed into line, and were made to march on in a more soldier-like manner."

Vehicles of every description, crowded with sick soldiers and citizens, and bound northwards, passed rapidly through the streets on this eventful morning. The contrabands flocked through them, each with his little bundle; and whole families of negroes, some of them with packs strapped on head and shoulders, little children almost too small to walk, and lean horses carrying two or three, went fol-

lowing the train. Meantime, the thunder of cannonading
had commenced. Nearer and nearer it came, and the cry
went forth that the Rebels were driving the Federal forces.
As the fugitives retired from the city, they looked back
and beheld flames ascending from many of the buildings, in which military stores and powder had been contained, and to which the torch had been applied to prevent
them falling into the hands of the Rebels. Here was por-
trayed a vivid illustration of the horrors of war. Homes
that once had been the abodes of happiness, now became
desolate, and fell a prey to the ravages of the flames. The
town in which but two months previous the Federals had
entered with joyous hearts, treading to the sound of martial music, and under the shadow of their waving banners,
they now left in despondency, and with the marks of fear
depicted in their faces.

We will now return to the rear. Two hours past midnight on Saturday the two brigades under the command of
Colonels Gordon and Donnelly, upon whom, toward the
close of the day, had devolved the duty of protecting the
end of the column, and who had thus far succeeded in keeping the Confederates at bay, halted for the night in the outskirts of Winchester. The men went into bivouac without fire, with but little food, and completely exhausted.

At Winchester all doubts as to the number of the Confederate forces were set at rest. All classes—secessionists,
Unionists, refugees, fugitives, and prisoners—agreed that

it was overwhelming, and that from twenty-five to thirty thousand men were in close proximity to the place. Rebel officers who came into the Federal camp with entire unconcern, supposing that their own troops occupied the town, confirmed these statements, and added that an attack would be made on the National forces at daybreak. Measures were, therefore, promptly taken to repel the attack; and at early dawn the two brigades in question were under arms. Soon after four o'clock, the artillery opened its fire, which was continued without intermission until the close of the engagement. Colonel Gordon's brigade was placed on the right of the line, and was partly covered from the fire of the enemy by stone walls. Colonel Donnelly's brigade was assigned to the left. The earliest movement of the Rebels was in this direction, but this being intercepted by a detachment of cavalry, it was apparently abandoned.

The main body of the Confederates was hidden during the early part of the action by the crest of a hill, and the woods in the rear. Their force was apparently masked on the Federal right, and their manœuvres indicated a purpose to turn it upon the Berryville road, where it appeared subsequently that they had placed a considerable force with a view of preventing reünforcements arriving from Harper's Ferry. In this, however, they were frustrated until a small portion of the National troops under the erroneous impression that an order had been given to withdraw, made a movement to the rear. No sooner was this observed by the Rebels than their regiments swarmed upon the crest of the hill, and advanced from the woods upon the Federal right, which fell back upon the town, continuing its fire by the way.

The overwhelming force of the Confederates thus suddenly showed itself. It was considered unwise to make further resistance, and orders were given to the entire Federal force to withdraw, which was done in good order. A portion of the troops passed through the town in some confusion, but the column was soon re-formed, and continued its march.

This engagement held the Rebels in check for five hours. The forces were greatly unequal, there being not less than twenty-five thousand of Jackson's troops in position, and capable of being brought into action, whilst the two brigades of Federals consisted of less than four thousand men. The latter were, however, assisted by nine hundred cavalry, ten Parrott guns, and a battery of six-pounders.

This battle took place upon nearly the same spot on which the previous battle of Winchester had been fought; but when we take into consideration, the great disparity in the forces which met in deadly encounter on the occasion of this second engagement, it can scarcely be admitted that the Confederate commander here regained all the laurels which he had here lost.

The Federals now continued their march in three parallel columns, and proceeded in the direction of Martinsburgh.

The Confederates pursued them with promptitude and vigor, but the movements of the retreating party were now rapid and without loss. Halting for two hours and a half at Martinsburgh, they proceeded on their way to the banks of the Potomac, and the rear-guard reached that river at sundown—forty-eight hours after the first news of the attack upon Front Royal. Thus was completed a march of fifty-three miles, thirty-five of which had been performed in one day.

"The scene of the river," says General Banks in his report, "when the rear-guard arrived, was of the most animating and exciting description. A thousand camp-fires were burning on the hill-side, a thousand carriages of every description were crowded upon the banks, and the broad river between the exhausted troops and their coveted rest."

On the following morning, the entire force was moved across the river in safety, and, remarks the Federal Commander "There never were more grateful hearts in the same number of men, than when, at mid-day on the twenty-sixth, we stood on the opposite shore."

The entire number of men lost by this retreat was estimated at about nine hundred, of whom thirty-eight were killed, one hundred and fifty-five wounded, and seven hundred and eleven missing. Of the wagon-train which consisted of nearly five hundred wagons, General Banks states that he only lost fifty-five, and that these with but few exceptions were all burned on the road, and not abandoned to the enemy. He further states that nearly all his supplies were saved with the exception of the stores lost at Front Royal and at Winchester, at which latter place a considerable portion was destroyed by his own troops.

The Confederates consider this expedition of General Jackson to have been a most glorious one, and they find reason to ascribe its results to the zeal, heroism, and genius of its Commander alone. They claim for it a comparison with some of the most famous campaigns in modern history. It was brief but brilliant, only three weeks having passed between the commencement of the aggressive movement, and the expulsion of the Federal army from the valley of Virginia. During this short period it is claimed that Jackson fought four battles and had a number of skirmishes, killed and wounded a considerable number of the Federals, captured four thousand prisoners, secured millions of dollars' worth of stores, destroyed many millions of dollars' worth for the Federals, recovered Winchester, and annihilated the invading army of the valley — and all this with a loss scarcely exceeding one hundred in killed and wounded.

We leave it to the reader to compare these statements with those made by the commander of the National forces, and to draw his own deductions therefrom.

# CHAPTER VII.

As we have already stated, the retreat of General Banks
led to the wildest excitement in the cities of the North.
In Baltimore this excitement culminated in acts of violence,
and prominent citizens who were tainted with Secession
proclivities were publicly mobbed in the streets, and their
lives placed in jeopardy. The Administration not only
found itself necessitated to make a call upon the country
for additional troops, but it required the Governors of
several of the loyal States to forward detachments of their
militia for the protection of the National Capital.

It now became a part of the Federal plan to outflank
Jackson and to capture him with his entire force, before
he could return to his base of operations. For this purpose General Fremont was instructed to advance from
Franklin, in the Mountain Department, where his force

was now located, and enter the valley, from the west, in the neighborhood of Strasburgh; whilst General Shields was sent from the Rappahannock to reach the same point *via* Manassas Gap on the east.

General Jackson, learning of these movements, hastened from his advanced position on the line of the Potomac, and rapidly retraced his steps up the valley, with the hope of eluding his pursuers, and reaching the upper end thereof before they would be enabled to intercept him. Before doing this, however, he made an attempt to dislodge the National forces at Harper's Ferry, but failed to accomplish his object. For two days he endeavored to draw them out from their stronghold, so that he could give them battle on ground of his own choosing; but General Saxton, who was then in command of the Federal troops there stationed, would not be lured by the wiles of his scheming foe. Foiled in these attempts, Jackson determined to storm the place. This he did about nightfall on Friday, May the thirtieth, amid a terrific storm. The scene at the time was very impressive. The night was intensely dark; the hills around were alive with the signal-lights of the Rebels; the rain descended in torrents; vivid flashes of lightning illuminated, at intervals, the magnificent scenery; while the crash of thunder, echoing among the mountains, drowned into comparative insignificance the roar of the artillery.

After an action of about one hour's duration, the Confederates retired. They made another unsuccessful attack at

4*

midnight, and after a short engagement disappeared. Jackson then retreated. On the following morning the Federals pursued him as far as Charlestown, only to learn that his rear-guard had passed through the place an hour before their arrival.

On the morning of the day that this affair took place at Harper's Ferry, a portion of Jackson's forces stationed at Front Royal were driven from that place by a brigade of National troops. The Rebels were taken as completely by surprise as Colonel Kenly's command had been the week previous, and they had no time left either to save or destroy any thing. Railroad engines and cars filled with stores, along with many prisoners, fell into the hands of the Federals, and several of the Union men who were here captured by the Confederates, on their attacking the place, were recaptured.

General Fremont left Franklin on Sunday, May the twenty-fifth, and his advance-guard entered Strasburgh on the evening of the following Sunday, the troops having halted one day on the road, being compelled to do so from exhaustion. The march was made amid heavy rains, which rendered the roads almost impassable.

With the exception of a small skirmish, which occurred at Wardensville, the advancing party met with no opposition to their progress, until the morning of the day on which they reached Strasburgh. On this morning, however, Colonel Cluseret's brigade, which formed the advance guard of Fremont's army, had a sharp encounter and brisk cannonading with Jackson's rear-guard or flanking column. Although the latter were repulsed, after an engagement of two hours' duration, they had been enabled to gain time for and to protect Jackson's main force, which was then hurriedly retreating over the road from Winchester to Strasburgh.

Jackson had pushed on his forces so swiftly that he succeeded in reaching Strasburgh just in season to pass between Fremont on the one side and Shields on the other. The advance-guard of the former entered Strasburgh on the evening of the day that Jackson passed through the town, whilst Shields's advance-guard reached it the following morning. Shields's advance-guard now joined Fremont's force, whilst his main army passed up the valley to the eastward.

The Federals were now close upon Jackson's heels, and the Confederate rear-guard now found it necessary on many occasions to dispute the progress of the National forces. General Ewell was in the command of this rear-guard, and received able assistance from Ashby's cavalry. During the passage of the Union soldiers, they found strewn along the roads and in the adjoining woods, such relics as a fugitive army is wont to scatter in its trail; and dead, wounded, and exhausted soldiers lay by the side of the road.

Woodstock was reached on Monday night by the Federals, Jackson's army having passed through the town on the same day. The Confederates were so closely pressed that their bridge-burners could but half accomplish the task which was allotted to them, and the Federals were easily able to repair any damage which the bridges sustained at their hands. However, at Mount Jackson, the long bridge which there crosses the Shenandoah, a river too swift and deep to be forded, was so far destroyed as seriously to delay the Federals in their onward progress. Upon reaching this point Jackson was so closely pressed that his rearguard had but barely passed over one end of the bridge, when the Federal cavalry were about to enter upon the other.

On, on, Jackson sped, much delayed in his progress by the exhaustion of his troops, and the breaking down of his trains, and sorely pressed by the advancing forces of his pursuers. On June the sixth he had another severe encounter with the National troops in a woody district in the southern outskirts of the town of Harrisonburgh. In this engagement he first obtained a slight advantage, owing to the mismanagement of Colonel Windham, who had the command of such of the Federal forces as were brought into action. The ground lost by this repulse to the National troops was, however, speedily regained by General Bayard, who made a vigorous attack upon the Rebels, and ultimately drove them back, and compelled them to renew their retreat. In this engagement the distinguished Rebel General Ashby, who covered the retreat with his whole cavalry force and three regiments of infantry, and who exhibited admirable skill and audacity, was killed.

On June the eighth the two armies came into collision at Cross Keys, seven miles beyond Harrisonburgh. Although Jackson had a much superior force to Fremont, throughout his retreat he had studiously avoided fighting a pitched battle, as he was fearful that the delay which would be caused thereby would prevent him from escaping the large force which was marching to the eastward, under the command of General Shields, to outflank him. General Fremont was consequently the attacking party on this occasion. The battle took place on a Sunday, and the day was one of those bright and glorious ones which, at this period of the year, so intoxicate with their freshness, and so elevate the spirits. It is said that battles commenced on a Sunday are seldom successes for the attacking party, and we fear that we can not claim this battle as any exception to the general rule.

Having upon the previous evening, and upon that morning, caused reconnoissances to be made with a view of ascertaining the position of the Rebels, General Fremont approached them about eleven o'clock, and the advance soon opened that preliminary fire which usually precedes a general engagement. The face of the country in this district is rolling, and covered at various points with woods, generally of oak, from the size of a small sapling to that of a man's body. The ground on which the battle was fought is a succession of hillocks, on which several farms stretch out for two or three miles from north to south, and form a belt of cleared land, which is lowest in the centre and gradually rises as the timber is approached in either direction. To the north, as if standing sentinel and gravely looking down upon the scene, rises a lofty mountain-peak, its top enveloped in a blue haze, and its steep sides bathed in the sunlight of a beautiful morning. Far off to the east, stretching up and down the Shenandoah, the distant peaks of the Blue Ridge form a background of indescribable beauty.

The attack was commenced by General Fremont's right, the line of which extended for nearly a mile and a half. The Rebels were here driven back, and in this quarter the chances of success were strongly in favor of the Federals, until an order was given for this wing to withdraw slowly and in good order from the position it had gained, and proceed to the relief of the left, which had suffered severely from the fire of the Confederates.

On the left General Stahl's German brigade, whilst in the act of ascending a slope as they were about proceeding to the attack, were opposed by a murderous fire from the Rebels, which produced sad havoc and caused their ranks to be terribly thinned. They were consequently compelled to fall back. Some mountain howitzers were then directed upon the Rebels; the cannonading became furious; the deep thunders of the artillery reverberated through the valley; the sharp crash of musketry rang through the woods; shells went screaming on the errand of death; and the cloud of sulphurous smoke which hung like a funeral pall over the advancing and receding waves, told too well the work of carnage and death then going on.

Had Stahl been enabled to advance but a few feet farther, his troops would have had an opportunity to pour into the Rebels a fire which would have driven them before him. This, with the combined movement of the Federal troops on the right, and of those which already had penetrated the centre, would doubtless have swept Jackson's entire line, would have put him to rout, would have captured his guns, and would have gained a most complete victory for the National forces. But this was prevented by the mistake of an order, which had been forwarded to some regiments directing them to relieve the advancing party, having been construed into one to retire.

The misfortune of this misunderstanding can scarcely be estimated. One more effort and the regiments which had forced themselves right up to the Rebel guns would doubtless have gained a splendid triumph. But the opportunity was lost, and General Jackson again slipped through the fingers of the Federals, after Fremont had for fifteen days marched his army through wind and rain to catch him.

There was for a time a lull in the storm—each party seeming satisfied to take a rest. Then in retiring, Jackson sent a few shells which fell in the midst of General Fremont's staff, and caused them to scatter far and wide. These compliments were returned, and a brisk artillery duel was kept up for a short time, and then all again was quiet. Night came on, the clouds of smoke which had obscured the sky disappeared, and the moon smiled down as peacefully upon the scene where carnage had held high carnival as if no ghastly features, pale in death, were there.

On the following morning General Fremont again marched with his troops in pursuit. They had not proceeded far before they reached Mill Creek Church, which had been used as a hospital by the Rebels, and in which they found several wounded Union soldiers. "Let it be said to the Rebels' credit," writes a gentleman who was present at the time, "that they treated our wounded humanely. Many left upon the field had blankets thrown over them and canteens of water placed by their side, while they nearly all say that they were as well treated as the Rebels themselves."

The Federal loss in the battle of Cross Keys was about one hundred and twenty-five killed, and five hundred wounded. General Fremont states that upward of two hundred of the Confederates were counted dead in one field, and that many others were scattered through the woods. Several more of the dead and the entire of Jackson's wounded had been removed in wagons under cover of the night.

On the same day that the battle of Cross Keys was being fought, a minor action took place at Port Republic between the train-guard of Jackson's army and a small Federal force belonging to General Shields's division, and under the command of Colonel Carroll. This resulted in the repulse of the latter; the forces engaged being more than two to one against him. On the following day occurred the battle of Port Republic.

While General Fremont was closely pressing Jackson in the rear, a portion of General Shields's command, under General Tyler, was moving on the east in advance of the main column, with the intention of reaching Waynesboro, on the Virginia Central Railroad, for the purpose of destroying the railroad, and thus cutting off Jackson's line of communication by that route with Gordonsville and Richmond. The troops under Colonel Carroll formed the advance-guard of this force. Jackson was well aware of this plan to intercept him, and to frustrate it he brought into operation that celerity of movement for which he was so celebrated.

After Colonel Carroll's repulse on the Sunday, he fell back to and joined the troops under General Tyler. It was a part of General Shields's instructions to these officers that they should destroy the long bridge which crosses the Shenandoah at Port Republic, and by this means cut off Jackson's retreat at this point also. This, however, they were prevented from accomplishing.

Jackson, continuing his retreat, reached Port Republic on the morning of the ninth, when he immediately despatched a force to attack General Tyler. This force was repulsed, but on reenforcements being received, the Confederates drove back the Federals and captured their guns, which could not be removed, owing to the horses having been killed or disabled, and the roads being so heavy that it was impossible for the men to drag them through the deep mud.

During this time General Fremont's army moved in the direction of Port Republic without opposition. As it drew near the place a dense volume of smoke was seen rising in the air. The troops pressed on to discover the cause, but reached the river just as the last Rebel had crossed the Shenandoah; arriving, however, in time to observe Jackson's interminable train winding along like a huge snake in the valley beyond. Several Rebel regiments were drawn in line of battle on the opposite side of the Shenandoah. An unfordable river lay between the opposing armies, and the bridge was in flames.

Thus ended the Federal pursuit of the fleet-footed Jackson. General Fremont had left Franklin on Sunday, May the twenty-fifth, taking up his line of march for the Valley of Virginia. At Petersburgh he had left his tents and heavy baggage. With one exception, he had marched sixteen consecutive days. The rains had been heavy and severe, and the soldiers had been compelled to bivouac in water and mud, lying down in their drenched clothes to obtain a few hours' rest, so that they might be enabled to endure the fatigues of the coming day. Transportation had been difficult. Forage and provisions had been scarce, for the country had been swept clear thereof by former armies. Sometimes the soldiers had but a short allowance of bread;

sometimes they had none, whilst some of them had worn
out their shoes, and were compelled to march barefooted.
However, they endured these trials with great patience.
Under circumstances such as these, and after seven days
of almost continuous skirmishing, was fought the battle of
Cross Keys. It has been argued that if General Fremont
had closely followed Jackson after this battle, the latter
would have been attacked in both front and rear, and he
would thus have been prevented from making good his
escape. The prostration of the Federal troops from the
causes which we have here related may possibly have been
a barrier to this desirable consummation.

It is much to be regretted that, during General Fremont's progress, some of his troops had conducted themselves in a manner that necessitated their commander to
issue an order, calling their attention to the many disor-
ders and excesses and the wanton outrages upon property
which had marked their line of march from Franklin to
Port Republic. He considered that the magnitude of the
evil should be summarily and severely checked. He, therefore, threatened severe punishment for any similar offences
that might occur in future. The men had entered dwell-
ings and appropriated to themselves property of various
kinds which fell in their way. It was stated that the
Germans were the greatest offenders, but witnesses to
these excesses state that these men were too often made
the scapegoats for the offences of their comrades of American birth.

After Jackson had made his escape from his pursuers, he proceeded toward Stewardsville, passed through the Gap of the Blue Ridge mountains, and thence, *via* Gordonsville, to Richmond, there to take his part in the battles which were to relieve that city from the presence of a besieging army.

The state in which this charming Valley of Virginia was left by the contending armies of the North and the South, after they had trodden and retrodden its fertile fields, and after they had passed through and pillaged its pleasant towns, is thus pictured by one who was an eye-witness to the desolation which war had left behind :

"A more beautiful country than this Valley of the Shenandoah God's sun never smiled on. The scenery is magnificent, but not with sterile peaks and frowning rocks. Green vestured fields and gentle, round-bosomed hills nestle down in the arms of great mountains, and you know they are quick with growing life, even while they slumber. It rather moves me to sympathy to see the trail of devastation that the two armies have left after them. Meadows of clover are trodden into mud ; the tossing plumes of the wheat-fields along the line of march are trodden down, as though a thousand reaping-machines had passed over and through them. Dead horses lie along the road, entirely overpowering the sweet scent of the clover-blossoms, and flinging out upon the air a more villainous stench than could by any possibility ascend from the left wing of the Tartarian pit. Fences are not, landmarks have vanished, and all is one common waste."

Before the war this Valley was dotted with happy homes, but the curtain had not descended upon this, the second act of the bloody drama, before these homes were tenantless, and their former peaceful occupants were scattered like chaff before the piercing blast of the pitiless storm.

# CHAPTER VIII.

## THE SEVEN DAYS' BATTLES BEFORE RICHMOND.

Jackson created a Major-General—McClellan Lands upon the Peninsula—
Occupation of Yorktown—Williamsburgh—Hanover Court-House—Seven
Pines—Fair Oaks—Stuart's celebrated Raid—Position and Number of·
the Opposing Forces—FIRST DAY: Battle of Oak Grove—Confederate
Council of War—SECOND DAY: Battle of Mechanicsville—THIRD DAY:
Battle of Gaines's Mill—The Battle-Ground—Jackson's Attack on the
Federal Rear—The River Crossed by the Federal Right Wing—Council
of War—FOURTH DAY: Battle of Garnett's Farm—FIFTH DAY: Battle of
Peach Orchard—Battle of Savage's Station—SIXTH DAY: Battle of White
Oak Swamp—Battle of Glendale—SEVENTH DAY: Battle of Malvern Hill—
Losses of the Combatants—Importance of Jackson's Services during the
Week.

IMMEDIATELY after Jackson had foiled his pursuers in
the Valley of Virginia, he hastened to unite his forces
with those which were guarding the Confederate capital
against the grand attack of General McClellan's army, then
daily anticipated. Jackson steps upon this scene in the
character of a Major-General, having been advanced to
that position in consequence of the great military abilities
which he had exhibited during the Valley campaign just
terminated.

Before entering into the particulars of the seven days' battles, it is advisable that we should refresh the reader's memory by referring to a few of the leading events which preceded this week—a week so terribly prominent in the calendar of our history.

It having been conceived that Richmond could be more easily reached by the army of the Potomac if it traversed the Peninsula, and took advantage of the communication by water which it possessed, instead of having to cross the numerous rivers which intercept the road by Fredericksburgh, it was resolved to adopt the former route to the Rebel capital. General McClellan having made all his arrangements for the removal of his vast army from the Potomac to the vicinity of Fortress Monroe, in the middle of March issued a spirited and cheerful address to his troops, in which he informed them that the "period for inaction" had passed, and that he was about "to bring them face to face with the Rebels."

At the beginning of April, he had landed his forces upon the eastern point of the Peninsula, and immediately commenced moving upon Yorktown. He found that place strongly fortified, and it was not until the fourth of May that he obtained possession of it, the Rebels having evacuated the place during the preceding night. Before this time, the troops under General McDowell—upon which McClellan depended for assistance, by a flank movement at the head of the York River either encircling the Confederate forces or forcing them to retreat farther up the Peninsula—were removed from his command, to which cause has been attrib-

nted the delay that occurred in the occupation of Yorktown.

Following the retreating Rebels, McClellan came into collision with them on May the fifth, at Williamsburgh, where
they stoutly contested his farther progress. From this place
they were finally expelled, but the action resulted in great
loss to the Federal forces, and at one period thereof it
was decidedly in favor of the Confederates. On the following day, a minor action occurred at the head of the York
River, where a force of Federals who had landed there were
driven back under cover of their gunboats.

The Federal army now advanced toward the banks of the
Chickahominy, being, however, slightly impeded in its progress by repeated skirmishes with the Rebels. On the twenty-seventh of May, a portion of McClellan's right wing, under
command of General Fitz-John Porter, had an engagement
with them at Hanover Court-House, and after a sharp conflict succeeded in accomplishing the object of the mission, which was to cut off railroad communication between
Richmond and the North.

General Casey's division, which formed the left wing,
having crossed the Chickahominy, the Confederates took
advantage of a severe thunder-storm—which they trusted
would cause the river to be much swollen, and Casey's communication with the main body of the army thus cut off—to
attack this force on the thirty-first of May, at the Seven
Pines. The Confederates greatly outnumbered the Federals,
and would doubtless have totally annihilated the division

had it not been strongly reënforced. Some of the ground lost in the early part of the action was eventually regained, but at the close of the day the Rebels remained occupants of a portion of the Federal camp, and were in possession of several guns which they had captured. On the following morning the battle was resumed, when the Rebels were defeated and compelled to fall back upon Richmond. This second day's engagement is called the battle of Fair Oaks.

At this time McClellan was loudly calling for reënforcements, and it was naturally the object of the Confederates to prevent any addition to his forces. For this purpose, the latter planned Jackson's raid into the valley of the Shenandoah, which we have already described, and the successful accomplishment of which, Jackson was informed by his superiors, would be the greatest service he could render to his country.

Very little further of importance occurred until May the thirteenth, when the Confederate General J. E. B. Stuart, with a force of twelve hundred cavalry and a section of artillery, left the Rebel lines near Richmond, and as a feint moved as if he was proceeding to reënforce Jackson, but afterwards wheeled about and passed round the whole of the rear of the Union army, returning to his post on the fifteenth. During this dashing exploit, he took a number of prisoners, and captured stores to a large amount.

A brief reference to the situation of the opposing armies at the commencement of the seven days' contests, will here

5

be necessary to enable the reader to thoroughly understand the movements. If he will take a map of Virginia, and run his eye along the Virginia Central Railroad until it crosses the Chickahominy at the point designated as the Meadow Bridge, he will be in the vicinity of the position occupied by the extreme right of the Federal army. Tracing from this position a semi-circular line which crosses the Chickahominy in the neighborhood of the New Bridge, and then the York River Railroad, further on, he arrives at a point south-east of Richmond, but a comparatively short distance from the James River, where rests the Federal left. To be a little more explicit, let the reader spread his fingers so that their tips will form as near as possible the arc of a circle. Imagine Richmond as situated on his wrist; the outer edge of the thumb as the Central Railroad, the inner edge as the Mechanicsville turnpike; the first finger as the Nine-Mile, or New-Bridge road; the second as the Williamsburgh turnpike, running nearly parallel with the York River Railroad; the third as the Charles City turnpike, (which runs to the southward of the White Oak Swamp;) and the fourth as the Darbytown road. Commanding these several avenues were the forces of McClellan. The Confederate troops, with the exception of Jackson's corps, occupied a similar but of course smaller circle immediately around Richmond; the heaviest body being on the centre, south of the York River Railroad.

It will thus be seen that the Federal troops were situated on both sides of the Chickahominy, whilst the Confederates were confined exclusively to the right bank, scarcely a single scout crossing the stream. At the commencement of the siege—which may be considered to have extended from the twenty-second to the twenty-fifth of June—three Federal corps were stationed upon the Richmond side of the river, and two corps with General Stoneman's command on the other. One corps of the latter afterward crossed toward Richmond, making four upon that side, and General Mc-Call's division of Pennsylvania Reserves, which arrived on June the eighteenth, were added to the force which remained on the left bank. The left corps was commanded by General Keyes, and the rest, following in rotation toward the right, by Generals Heintzelman, Sumner, Franklin, and Porter, the latter's corps being that situated upon the left bank of the river, with its extreme right resting upon Meadow Bridge, about four miles north of Richmond, and formed the nearest approach of the Federal force to the Confederate capital.

The Confederate army consisted of eight grand divisions, each of which corresponded to a Federal army corps. These were commanded by Generals Huger, D. H. Hill, Longstreet, Smith, Magruder, A. P. Hill, Rains, and Ewell. Huger was stationed opposite the Federal left wing, and the others along to the right, in the order in which we have given their names. General Jackson, upon his arrival, was assigned to the extreme left of the Confederate army, where Stuart's cavalry was also stationed. He was thus placed in juxtaposition to Franklin's corps on the Federal right.

During the month of June the Confederate army was strongly reënforced from the West and South-west, as well as by Jackson's troops, and their forces in and around Richmond, at the commencement of the seven days' battles, have been variously estimated at from two hundred to two hundred and fifty thousand men, but we conclude that one hundred and fifty thousand will more nearly approach the actual number. To meet this vast force, General McClellan could not at the time muster more than eighty-six thousand men.

### FIRST DAY—OAK GROVE.

Though Wednesday, June the twenty-fifth, was the day upon which the seven days' battles before Richmond commenced, the operations on that day, so far as regarded the Confederates, were merely defensive. It was not until Thursday that the latter commenced those offensive proceedings which they anticipated would, and which actually did, remove from the vicinity of their capital the National forces so determinedly bent on its capture.

Information was received on Tuesday that General Jackson, with his own troops, along with those of Ewell and Whiting, was at Frederick's Hall, and that it was his intention to attack the Federal right flank and rear, in order to cut off McClellan's communication with the White House, and to throw the right wing of his army into the Chickahominy. The raid made by Stuart had induced the Federal commander to provide against this contingency, and he had consequently ordered to the James River, now relieved from the presence of the fearful Merrimac, a number of transports laden with commissary, quartermaster, and ordnance stores. General Stoneman was at the same time placed in charge of the cavalry on the right, with instructions to keep a vigilant watch over Jackson, and to give immediate information of any advance of the Rebels from that direction.

The right being thus guarded, General Heintzelman was directed to drive in the Confederate pickets in the woods from their front, in order to give the National forces command of cleared fields still farther in advance. This object was gallantly accomplished, although stubbornly resisted, the fighting falling principally on Hooker's division. The engagement took place at Oak Grove, about a mile in advance of the battle-field at Fair Oaks, and continued throughout the entire day of the twenty-fifth, commencing at nine o'clock in the morning and not terminating until ten o'clock at night. Just as the new line was gained, General McClellan was called from the field by intelligence which tended strongly to confirm the belief that Jackson was really approaching. Such, however, was not the case, but these repeated alarms are sufficient to prove with what fear any approach of the irresistless Rebel was viewed.

The Confederates being now in sufficient force to become the attacking party, they resolved upon ridding their capital from the presence of a besieging host. The plan proposed to be adopted having been thoroughly completed, a great council of war was being held at the Rebel headquarters, during the progress of the events which we have just narrated. In it were assembled nearly all that was eminent in the Rebel army. Johnston had been severely wounded at the battle of Seven Pines, and the mantle of the commander had fallen upon the shoulders of General Lee. Gazing cheerfully over the countenances of his comrades, for each of whom he had a part already assigned, the new commander stood like a rock. "Thoughtfully his eyes wandered from one to the other, as though he wished to stamp the features of each upon his memory, with the feeling that he, perhaps, should never behold many of them again. Close beside him towered the knightly form of General Baldwin; at his left leaned pensively Stonewall Jackson, the idol of his troops, impatiently swinging his sabre to and fro, as though the quiet room were too narrow for him, and he were longing to be once more at the head of his columns. A little aside, quietly stood the two Hills, arm in arm, while in front of them old General Wise was energetically speaking. Further to the right stood Generals Huger, Longstreet, Branch, Anderson, Whiting, Ripley, and Magruder, in a group. When all these generals had assembled, General Lee laid his plans before them, and in a few stirring words pointed out to each his allotted task. The scheme had already been elaborated. It was compact, concentrated action, and the result could not fail to be brilliant. When the conference terminated, all shook hands and hastened away to their respective army corps, to enter upon immediate activity."*

The plan of battle developed by the Confederates was,

* Richmond Correspondent of the *Cologne Gazette.*

first, to make a vigorous flank movement upon the Federal extreme right, which was within a mile or two of the Central Railroad; secondly, as soon as they fell back to the next road below, the Rebel divisions there posted were to advance across the Chickahominy, charge front, and in co-operation with Jackson, who was to make a detour, and attack the Federals in flank and rear, drive them still further on; and finally, when they had reached a certain point, known as "The Triangle," embraced between the Charles City, New Market, and Quaker Roads, all of which intersect, these several approaches were to be possessed by the Confederates; the National forces were to be thus hemmed in and compelled either to starve, capitulate, or fight their way out with tremendous odds and topographical advantages against them. How this plan happened to fail, at least partially, in the execution, will appear in the course of our narrative.

Looking at the position of the two armies, it will be seen that the vantage ground lay with the Southern army, for General McClellan had his forces necessarily on both sides of the Chickahominy, and, owing to the many ravines in the neighborhood, he could not, without great difficulty and much loss of time, execute his military movements. His front line reached over a distance of more than twenty miles in the form of a semi-circle, extending from the vicincinity of the James River toward Richmond and Ashland. The heights on the banks of the Chickahominy were, however, so fortified that his army, notwithstanding the great length of its line, had excellent defensive cover. The Confederate army occupied the inner side of the semi-circle, and the various divisions thereof being more contiguous to each other than those of the Federal army necessarily could be, they were more readily able to assist each other, whenever, from force of circumstances, any assistance should be required.

### SECOND DAY—MECHANICSVILLE.

Thursday dawned, and the morning was clear but warm. Jackson was in motion as early as three o'clock. His *corps d'armée*, strengthened by the addition of Whiting's division, now consisted of about thirty thousand men. He moved by a forced march from Ashland, twenty miles distant from Richmond, for the purpose of commencing his outflanking operations.

At Hanover Court-House he threw forward General Branch's brigades between the Chickahominy and Pamunkey Rivers, to establish a junction with General A. P. Hill, who had to cross the stream at Meadow Bridge. Jackson then bore away from the Chickahominy, so as to gain ground toward the Pamunkey, marching to the left of Mechanicsville and toward Coal Harbor, while Hill, keeping well to the Chickahominy, approached Mechanicsville, and there engaged the National forces. This was shortly after mid-day. The fight was opened with artillery at long-range, but the Rebels discovering the Federal superiority in this arm, foreshortened the range and came into closer conflict. Previous to this, however whilst the shells of the

Confederates were not destructive in the intrenchments of the Federals, the gunners of the latter played upon the exposed ranks of the former with fearful effect. The fight increased in fury as it progressed, and it finally became the most terrible artillery combat that the war had thus far witnessed. The uproar was incessant and deafening for hours. No language can describe its awful grandeur. The Rebels at last essayed a combined movement. Powerful bodies of troops rushed forward to charge the Federal lines, but they were ruthlessly swept away. Again and again the desperate fellows were pushed at the breast-works only to be more cruelly slaughtered than before.

General McCall, whose division of Porter's corps was here engaged, in the mean time had his force strengthened by the brigades of Martindale and Griffin, of Morell's division. The volume of infantry firing was thus increased, and at dark, the Rebels retired from the contest, resigning the honor of the day to the Federals.

While the battle of Mechanicsville was in progress, another action took place at Ellyson's Mills, to the right or south-east of that place, and about a mile and a half distant therefrom; but the two engagements occurred so near to each other that they may be considered as part of the same battle. At this latter place, the Federals had a battery of sixteen guns situated on elevated ground, and defended by epaulements, supported by rifle-pits. Beaver Creek, about twelve feet wide and waist-deep, ran along the front and left flank of this position, while abattis occupied the space

5*

between the creek and the battery: General Lee ordered this battery to be charged, but his troops were unable to advance any nearer than the opposite side of the creek. The Rebels suffered very severely, during the engagement, and retired from the conflict about ten o'clock at night.

Another occurrence also took place on the twenty-sixth of June which is worthy of being recorded. Colonel Lansing was ordered to proceed with the Seventeenth New-York and Eighteenth Massachusetts regiments to Old Church, about six miles east of Mechanicsville, there to intercept General Jackson, who was on his way to cut off the Federal communications with the White House. Jackson succeeded in separating Lansing's communication with the right wing of the Federal army, at that time fighting on the banks of Beaver Creek. The latter, however, was ulti mately enabled to make his way to Tunstall's Station upon the railroad, and from thence to the York River, where he was taken up by the transports.

Whenever General Branch acted directly under General Jackson's command, he implicitly obeyed his instructions, and acted with energy and courage; but when he was out of his commander's sight, he became nervous and unresolved how to act. On the present occasion he failed to carry out the orders which Jackson had distinctly given to him, and instead of advancing boldly he hesitated, and delayed his march from hour to hour. General Hill sent his Aid-de-Camp during the battle to order up Branch's brigade, but the latter was not to be found, and he did not make his appearance on the battle-field until night had put an end to the contest.

It being now evident to General McClellan that Jackson was proceeding toward the Pamunkey, he considered that the position of his right wing was no longer tenable. He therefore determined to concentrate his forces, and withdrew Porter's command to a position near Gaines's Mill, where he could rest both his flanks on the Chickahominy, and cover the most important bridges over that stream. As it was also evident that Jackson was intent upon seizing the public property on the banks of the Pamunkey, and cutting off the Federal retreat in that direction, Stoneman's command was moved swiftly down to finish operations there, and orders were issued for the removal or destruction of all public stores at White House. Meantime all trains and equipages of the right wing were withdrawn during the night to Trent's Bluff on the right bank of the Chickahominy, and the wounded were conveyed to the hospital at Savage's Station — alas! there to be deserted to the enemy they had beaten. These movements indicated that there was danger in the distance.

### THIRD DAY—GAINES'S MILL.

By daylight on Friday morning, General McCall had fallen back in the rear of Gaines's Mill, and in front of Woodbury's bridge, where he was posted, his left joining the right of Butterfield's brigade, which rested on the woods and near to the swamps of the Chickahominy. Morell was on his right in the centre, and General Sykes's command, five thousand regulars, and Duryea's Zouaves, held the extreme right. The line occupied crests of hills, near the New Kent road, some distance east by south of Gaines's Mill. In addition to these changes, General Slocum's division, about eight thousand strong, was moved across the river to support Porter, as it was assumed that the Rebels would reappear in that quarter in stronger force than they had been on the previous day. General McClellan having received intelligence, in the course of the morning, that Longstreet's corps was at Mechanicsville, ready to move down on either bank of the Chickahominy, according to circumstances, this, with other threatening movements of the Rebels on various parts of the centre and left, placed a limit to the number of reenforcements for the support of Porter. Under these circumstances it was likewise impossible to withdraw him to the right bank of the river by daylight, especially as the enemy was so close upon him that the attempt could not have been made without severe loss, and would have placed the right flank and rear of the army at their mercy. It was consequently necessary to give battle upon and hold the position now occupied at any cost, and in the mean time perfect arrangements for the change of base to the James River.

Let us now impart to the reader a knowledge of the ground in the vicinity of Gaines's Mill. For this purpose we will approach the scene from the Confederate lines. Emerging from the woods, the road leads to the left and then to the right round Gaines's house, where the whole ground, for the area of about two miles, is an open, unbroken succession of undulating hills. Standing at the north door of the house, the whole country to the right, for the distance of one mile, is a gradual slope toward a creek, through which the main road runs up an open hill and then winds to the right. In front, to the left, are orchards and gulleys running gradually to a deep creek. Directly in front, for the distance of a mile, the ground is almost table-land, suddenly dipping to the deep creek mentioned above, and faced by a timber-covered hill which fronts the table-land. Beyond this timber-covered hill the country is again open and is a perfect plateau, with a farm-house and out-houses in the centre, and the main road winding to the right and through all the Federal camps. To the south-east of Gaines's house is a large tract of timber, commanding all advances upon the main road. In this timber a strong body of Federal skirmishers were posted with artillery, to annoy the Confederate flank and rear, should they advance upon the Federal camps by the main road or over the table-lands to the north.

Early in the morning a portion of Longstreet's corps drove back such of the Federals as had been left in the vicinity of Mechanicsville, the latter retiring upon their new defensive line. The Confederates shortly after advanced along the entire line in the following order of battle: Longstreet on the right, resting on the Chickahominy swamp; A. P. Hill on his left; then Whiting; then Ewell and Jackson's corps, under command of the latter general;

then D. H. Hill on the extreme left of the line, which extended in the form of a crescent beyond New Coal Harbor, on the north, and toward Baker's Mills on the south. The battle commenced about mid-day by the batteries of D. H. Hill opening a vigorous fire on the Federal right. He, however, soon found it impossible to hold his position, and his guns were soon silenced. Reënforced, he renewed the attack, but only to meet with a second repulse and considerable loss. A third attack met with no better success. The object, however, of the Confederates in this attempted flank movement on the right of the Federals was mainly intended to draw the attention of the latter from Longstreet's contemplated attack on their left.

The din of battle now veered round to the centre and the left. At about half-past three o'clock P.M., Longstreet commenced to drive the Federals down the Chickahominy. At four o'clock the battle raged with intense fury in the vicinity of Gaines's Mill, and upon the ground which we have described. Here the conflict lasted for nearly two hours. The columns surged backward and forward, first one yielding and then the other. The Federal centre made a desperate stand, but it was not until it had hurled its last fresh brigade against the Rebels that they were beaten back. The Confederates finding that they could not force the Federal centre, now threw their columns against its left. Here the roar of musketry increased in volume, and the conflict became more terrific as time sped on. The Confederates had suffered severely from the raking fire which the Federals had poured upon them from the plateau. The latter swept the whole face of the country with their artillery, and would have annihilated the Rebel force if it had not been screened by the inequalities of the land. The Rebels descended into the deep creek and passed up the hill beyond, but so terrific was the hail-storm of lead which fell thick and fast around them, that it was with great difficulty their regiments could be induced to withstand it. In fact, in one instance, one of their generals, sword in hand, threatened to behead the first man that hesitated to advance. The Federals were now compelled to withdraw their guns and take up a fresh position wherefrom to assail the foe, which was advancing from the woods and toward the plateau. Forward pushed the Confederates. Officers had no horses—all were shot. Brigadiers marched on foot, regiments were commanded by captains, and companies by sergeants; yet onward they rushed, with yells and colors flying, and backward, still backward fell the Federals. When the plateau was reached, the Confederates found in their front the Federal camps stretching far away to the north-east. Drawn up in line of battle were the commands of McCall and Porter and others. Banners darkened the air, and artillery vomited forth incessant volleys of grape, canister, and shell. Brigade after brigade of the Confederates was hurled against the Northern heroes. In vain did the brave Butterfield, with hat in hand, rally, cheer, and lead his men forward again and again. In vain did he cry, " Once more, my gallant men !" as a last rallying order. The opposing hosts were too strong to be withstood. They assailed him in front, flank, and rear, and compelled him to fall back.

The Federals now moved with the evident intention of flanking the Rebel force engaged on its left, but the latter pressed onward to the heart of the Federal position, and when the National troops had almost succeeded in carrying out their flanking operations, great commotion was heard in the woods. Volley after volley was repeated in rapid succession. These welcome sounds were recognized and cheered by the Rebels. "It is Jackson," they shouted, "on their right and rear!" Yes, two or three brigades of Jackson's corps had approached from Coal Harbor and flanked the National forces. The fighting now increased in its severity. Worked up to madness, the Confederates dashed forward at a run, and drove the Federals back with irresistible fury.

Wheeling their artillery from the front, the Federals turned part of it to break the Rebel left and save their own retreat. The earth trembled at the roar. Not one Confederate piece had as yet opened fire; all had thus far been done by the bullet and the bayonet. Onward pressed the Rebel troops, through camps upon camps, capturing guns, stores, arms, and clothing. They swept every thing before them. Presenting an unbroken, solid front, and closing in upon the Federals, they kept up an incessant succession of volleys upon their confused masses. There was but one "charge!" and from the moment that the word of command was given, "Fix bayonets! forward!" the Rebel advance was never stopped, despite the awful reception which it met.

"But where is Jackson?" was the universal inquiry. He had travelled fast and was heading the flying foe. As night closed in, all was anxiety for intelligence from him. At seven o'clock, just as the victory was complete, the distant and rapid discharges of cannon told that Jackson had fallen on the retreating columns. Far into the night his troops hung upon and harassed the hard-pressed National forces.

General Jackson had accomplished his flanking march without encountering any serious resistance. Hardly had he arrived at the position marked out for him, ere he sent his columns to the charge. Notwithstanding the difficulties and exertions of the march which his troops had executed on short allowance, he flung them at once upon the Federals. In vain was all the courage, all the bold manœuvring of the latter. Like a tempest, General Stuart and his cavalry swept down upon them, and hurled every thing to the earth that stood in their way. Although the Federals had at first made obstinate resistance, they ultimately lost ground and fell back, throwing away arms, knapsacks, blankets—in fine, every thing that would impede their flight. Jackson could with a clear conscience issue the order: "Enough for the day." None of the other generals had performed their task with such rapidity and such success as he, and therefore the fruits of his victory were unusually large. The booty was immense; but in a strategetic point of view, Jackson's success was of far greater importance, since it completely cut off General McClellan from his original base on the York River. When, therefore, the triumph of his arms became known at the Confederate headquarters, the rejoicings bordered on frenzy, and all counted with perfect certainty upon the destruction or capture of the entire Federal force.

With the close of the day terminated the terrible scene of strife.

The army of the Potomac now occupied a very singular position. One portion of it was situated on the south side of the Chickahominy, fronting Richmond, and confronted by General Magruder. The other portion was on the north side of the river, and had turned its back upon Richmond, and fronted destruction in the persons of Lee, Longstreet, Jackson, and the two Hills.

By this engagement, General Stoneman's command had been separated from the rest of the army. Upon the previous day he had been scouting near Hanover Court-House, and after doing all that he could in the contests of both days to harass the Rebel flank and rear, he retired to the White House, whence he proceeded down the Peninsula to Fortress Monroe.

During the night the final withdrawal of the Federal right wing across the Chickahominy was completed, without difficulty or confusion, a portion of the regular troops only remaining on the left bank until early on the following morning, when the bridges were burned, and the whole army concentrated on the right bank of the river.

During the evening of the twenty-seventh, General McClellan's determination to change his base to the James River was for the first time whispered abroad. The plan was naturally very much canvassed, and the movement was considered a most critical one, especially as it had to be taken under compulsion. The tents of General McClellan's headquarters, which had been pitched in Doctor Trent's field, near the bank of the river, were moved at dusk to Savage's Station, on the railroad. "At night, as the several brigades came over the bridge, and clustered on the borders of the swamp, one single tent stood on the hillside, and that was General McClellan's. At eleven o'clock a council of war was held in front of this tent, in which the General commanding, corps commanders, with their aids, among them the French Princes and the General of Engineers, took part. A large fire had been lighted just beyond the arbor in front, and its blaze lighted up the faces of the generals as they sat in the arbor, which formed a pavilion for the tent. The conference was long and seemingly earnest. This was the first council called by General McClellan since he took the field, and here he disclosed his plans of reaching the James River." *

Keyes's line, which was on the extreme left, resting on

* "Leaves from the Diary of an Army Surgeon," by Thomas T. Ellis, M.D.

White Oak Swamp, was extended during the night, and the Federal artillery and transportation trains were ordered to prepare to move forward. That night General Casey was also directed to destroy all public property at the White House which could not be removed; to transport the sick and wounded to a place of safety, and to retire himself and rejoin the army on the James River. Friday night was thus actively and mournfully passed. The troops were ignorant of the true position, and it was desirable to conceal the truth from them. It was feared that the Rebels would renew their attack on the following morning, and every preparation was made to resist them successfully. The defensive right of the Federals was disposed on Trent's Bluffs, where it was supposed that the crossing of the Rebels might be successfully opposed. The night of Friday, June the twenty-seventh, was gloomy, but it was felicity itself when compared with those of the following Saturday, Sunday, Monday, and Tuesday.

### FOURTH DAY—GARNETT'S FARM.

Saturday dawned hot and cheerless to the National forces. No sound of a hostile gun disturbed the dread stillness until nine o'clock. The profound quiet of the morning became almost oppressive, so great was the contrast between its calmness and the fiery storm of the previous day. Shortly after that hour, however, the ominous silence which prevailed was broken by an awful cannonade, which opened from two forts in Garnett's field—a battery at General Porter's old position, and another below it—on the left bank of the Chick-ahominy. The fire was terrible, and compelled the forces upon which it was launched to abandon the strongest natural position on the whole Federal line. The troops attacked fell back a few hundred yards to the woods and threw up breastworks out of range. The Rebels, content with their success, ceased firing, and quiet was not again disturbed that day. The silence of the Confederates was explained that night by a negro slave who had escaped from his master at headquarters in Richmond. He said a despatch had been sent by Jackson to Magruder, who remained in command in front of Richmond, expressed thus: "Be quiet. Every thing is working as well as we could desire." Ominous words!

Saturday was also marked by the capture of the Fourth New-Jersey (Stockton's) regiment, the Eleventh Pennsylvania, and the famous "Bucktails," with their regimental standards. Also by rapid and successful movements of Jackson and Stuart, between the Chickahominy and the Pamunkey, in which they took the York River Railroad, cut off McClellan's communication with his transports, and destroyed his line of telegraph. Meanwhile, measures were taken by the Federals to increase the number of bridges across the White Oak Swamp. The trains were set in motion early in the day, and they continued moving along the swamp day and night until all had passed. Endless streams of artillery trains, wagons, and funereal ambulances, poured down the roads from all the camps, and plunged into the narrow funnel which was now the only hope of escape. It was absolutely necessary for the salvation of the army and the cause, that the wounded and mangled heroes who lay moaning in physical agony in the hospitals, should be deserted and left in the hands of those against whom they had so bravely fought.

Another fearful night was spent, but it was without catastrophe. Officers were on horseback throughout the greater part of the night, ordering on the great caravan and its escorts. There was again no wink of sleep, nor peace of mind, for any who realized the peril of his country in those dread hours.

### FIFTH DAY—PEACH ORCHARD; SAVAGE'S STATION.

At daylight, General McClellan was on the road. Thousands of cattle and wagons, and immense trains of artillery, intermingled with infantry and cavalry, choked up the narrow road. Generals Sumner's, Heintzelman's, and Franklin's corps, under command of the first named, were left to guard the rear, with orders to fall back at daylight, and hold the enemy in check until night. At no point along the line were the Federals more than three fourths of a mile from the Confederates, whilst in front of Sedgwick's line, the latter were not over six hundred yards distant. It was therefore necessary to move with the greatest caution, so as to conceal from the enemy the nature of their movements. Fortunately, however, by skilful secresy, column after column was marched to the rear—Franklin first, Sedgwick next, then Richardson and Hooker, and lastly the knightly Kearny.

A mile had been swiftly traversed when these splendid columns quickly turned at bay. The Confederates, keen-scented and watchful, had discovered the retrograde movement, and quick as thought were swarming and yelling at their heels. They were quickly met by fearful volleys of musketry and artillery, and all who were left of the slaughtered Rebel column fled howling back. Fresh troops stepped forth, and they, too, were sent surging back, until finally the Confederates retreated, content to watch and wait a happier moment to assail that desperate front. This engagement, which lasted for four hours, took place at Peach Orchard. The Federal troops which were engaged in it, having held the position as long as was necessary, marched on to Savage's Station in order to concentrate with other corps.

Toward noon the line had retired several miles, and rested behind Savage's Station to destroy the public property which had accumulated there. A locomotive and a train of cars were started and sent plunging madly into the Chickahominy. Ammunition was exploded, and the match was applied to stores of every description, until nothing was left to welcome the Confederates, who were closely treading in the Federal footsteps.

The advancing column and all its mighty train was in due course of time swallowed up in the maw of the dreary forest. It swept onward, onward, fast and furious, like an avalanche. But the march was as orderly as on any ordinary occasion, only swifter.  It seemed marvellous that such caravans of wagons, artillery, horsemen, soldiers, camp-followers, and other *impedimenta* of an army should press through the narrow road with so little confusion.

The Confederates, under Magruder, pressed closely on the Federal rear.  After the latter retired from Peach Orchard, the former entered the camping-ground to find almost every thing of value either removed or destroyed.  The Rebels then followed on to Savage's Station, guided thither by the dense volume of smoke which was seen to issue from the woods, and betokened the destruction which was in progress.  Arriving at the station about four o'clock P.M., the Rebels made a furious onslaught on the Federal rear, commanded by General Heintzelman, which engagement raged hotly for about three hours.  The Federals held the Confederates in check, fighting and retiring until they reached White Oak Swamp.  Here the fight continued until darkness put an end to the contest.  This battle in the forests was a fearful one.  Long lines of musketry vomited forth their liquid fire, while nature, as if emulous of man's fury, flashed its lightnings and rolled its grand thunder over the distant domes of Richmond.  So mingled were the flash and roar of heaven's artillery with the fire and din of battle, that it was at times difficult to decide which was the power of God, and which the conflict of man.  No combination of the dreadful in art and the magnificent in nature was ever more solemnly impressive.  It was a Sunday battle.

The Federal rear crossed the swamp under cover of night, whilst the Confederates lay on their arms with the design of renewing the battle on the return of daylight. Whilst Magruder was busily engaged pressing the National forces on the south side of the Chickahominy, the ever-active Jackson and the redoubtable Stuart were not less active on the north. Dashing down to the White House, the latter succeeded in capturing an immense quantity of supplies, ammunition, ordnance, a balloon, the rolling-stock of the railroad, and fifteen hundred prisoners, besides burning several large transports at the wharves. It was during this day (Sunday) that the Confederates became alive to the fact that General McClellan had succeeded in eluding them, and that he had stolen a march of twelve hours on General Huger, who had been placed in a position on his flank to watch his movements. So confidently had the Rebels calculated upon capturing the Federal army, that they were greatly mortified at the discovery of the fact that they had been out-generalled.

### SIXTH DAY—WHITE OAK SWAMP; GLENDALE.

About midnight on Sunday the lights were still blazing at the Federal headquarters. The commander was yet working with unyielding devotion; aids were still riding fast, but all else was silent. Presently, and the prostrate soldiers were startled from their slumbers by what appeared to be the terrific uproar of battle. Again and again the thundering sound was heard. It rolled sublimely away

6

off on the borders of the Chickahominy. The Rebels have crossed the river and are destroying the Federal right wing in the darkness. Such was the general impression, but the illusion—a natural one when the sounds of cannon and of musketry are dinning in every ear—was speedily dispelled. A dark cloud appeared in the horizon, and approached nearer and nearer, until at last it hung like a canopy over the black forest, and above the weary warriors.

Monday morning beamed like its predecessor, brilliantly and hotly. Until this day the Confederates evidently had proceeded upon the supposition that General McClellan was intending to retire to the Pamunkey, and the appearance in the north of the Federal cavalry and infantry—which we have already alluded to as having been severed from the rest of the army whilst watching the movements of Jackson—served to impress the Rebels with this idea. It was plain by this time, however, that the Federal intentions had become apparent to the Rebels, but the trains had been hurried on so rapidly that they had now nearly passed the point at which the latter could make any flank movement upon them.

At daybreak the Rebels resumed the pursuit of their flying foes. The troops of Generals D. H. Hill, Whiting, Ewell, and Jackson, under the command of General Jackson, crossed the Chickahominy and followed the Federals on their track by the Williamsburgh road and Savage's Station. Generals Longstreet, A. P. Hill, Huger, and Magruder at the same time proceeded by the Charles City road on the south, with the intention of cutting them off. Jackson came up with the Federal rear about eleven o'clock, at White Oak Swamp. The Federals had crossed the swamp and the bridge had been destroyed, and their artillery was posted so as to command the road and the crossing. Jackson ordered his artillery to be brought forward, under cover of a hill on the north bank of the swamp, and then to be thrown rapidly upon its crest and suddenly open fire upon the Federal batteries. This was about noon. The artillery duel which then commenced and continued with great spirit and determination until night closed the scene, was probably the most severe fight of field artillery which has taken place during the war. Jackson made some desperate efforts to cross the creek, but he was repulsed and kept back by General Smith's brigade, while the main body of Heintzelman's corps passed on toward the James River.

General A. P. Hill, who in the absence of Longstreet commanded the troops moving upon the Charles City road, came up with the Federals about five o'clock in the afternoon, at the Cross-roads, or Glendale, where he attacked Heintzelman's corps on the flank with much fierceness. During the evening the gunboats Aroostook and Galena, on the James River, got in range of the Confederate masses advancing from Richmond, and opened upon them with fearful havoc, the direction in which they should fire having been indicated by the signal corps. The Rebels were finally repulsed by a vigorous charge led by

General Heintzleman in person. The loss on both sides of this engagement was very great. Portions of nearly all the Federal corps were engaged, and Generals McCall and Reynolds were taken prisoners. The Confederate forces in action were A. P. Hill's and Longstreet's, commanded by the former. Magruder did not arrive until the battle was over, when he moved upon and occupied the battle-field, General Hill's troops being almost prostrated from their long and toilsome fight, and from their tremendous losses.

The Confederate President was on the field during the day, and had a narrow escape. He had taken a position in a house near the scene, when he was advised by General Lee to leave it at once, as it was threatened with danger. He had scarcely complied with the advice before the house was literally riddled with shell from the Federal batteries.

### SEVENTH DAY—MALVERN HILL.

By an early hour on Tuesday morning General McClellan had concentrated the entire of his forces at Malvern Hill, and in close proximity to the James River. The troops were placed in position to offer battle to the Rebels should they renew the attack, the left of the line resting on the admirable position of Malvern Hill, with a brigade in the low ground to the left, watching the road to Richmond. The line then followed a line of heights nearly parallel to the river, and bent back through the woods nearly to the James River on the right. General McClellan relied on the left for the natural advantages of the position. On the right, where the natural strength was less, some little cutting of timber was done, and the roads blocked. Although the Federal force was small for so extensive a position, its commander considered it necessary to hold it at any cost.

Tuesday, the first of July, was not a cheerful day for the Federals. The prospect was not a pleasant one. The Prince de Joinville, always gay and active as a lad, and always where there was battle, had gone. The Count de Paris, heir to the Bourbon throne, and the Duke de Chartres, his brother—the two chivalric and devoted aids to General McClellan, on whose courage, fidelity, intelligence, and activity he safely relied, and who served with him to learn the art of war—suddenly, without previous warning, took passage on a gunboat, and fluttered softly down the river. Two officers of the English army, who had also accompanied the Federal commander, and who had intended to remain with the army until Richmond was captured, announced their intention to leave in the first boat. These departures were at least ominous. The paymasters were advised to deposit their treasure on a gunboat. People looked gloomy. It had been stated that by the time the army reached Malvern Hill, the river at that point would be full of transports. On Monday, at noon, there was not one there, excepting a schooner laden with hay. By Tuesday evening, however, several steamers and a few forage-boats had arrived.

On Tuesday morning the Confederates renewed their pursuit. The divisions of D. H. Hill, Whiting, Ewell, and Jackson—the three latter under the command of Jackson—crossed the White Oak Bridge, Hill's division being to the right and Jackson's to the left. About three o'clock in the afternoon, they took their position to the left of the Rebel line, Longstreet, A. P. Hill, Magruder, and Huger, forming the right. In this order they advanced toward the lines of the Federals under the fire of artillery from land and water. Shortly after four o'clock, the rage of battle commenced. For an hour and a half battery after battery and regiment after regiment were advanced to the front, to be in turn driven back by the iron hail of the Federal artillery and the tremendous projectiles showered forth by the National gunboats. During this time, the indomitable Jackson assailed the Federals with that energy which he was ever wont to display.

Great was the slaughter in the Rebel ranks, and fruitless was their attempt to dislodge the Federals from the position they held, and where they had chosen to turn at bay and give battle to their eager pursuers. The sun of the first of July set upon the retiring columns of the Confederate host, and when night came on the final battle of the Peninsular campaign had become a matter of history.

Let us picture to the reader the appearance of this battle-field, as it met the eye a few days after the termination of the strife. The entire district appeared as if the lightnings of heaven had scathed and blasted it. The forests showed, in the splintered branches of a thousand trees, the fearful havoc of the artillery. The houses were riddled, the fences utterly demolished, the earth itself ploughed up in many cases for yards. Here stood a dismantled cannon, there a broken gun-carriage. Thick and many were the graves, the sods over which bore the marks of the blood of their occupants. On the plateau, across whose surface for hours the utmost fury of the battle raged, the tender corn that had grown up as high as the knee betrayed no sign of having ever laughed and sung in the breeze of early summer. Every thing, in short, but the blue heavens above, spoke of the carnival of death which had been there so frightfully celebrated.

It is needless to state that the losses on both sides in the seven days' battles were very great. The Federal loss in killed, wounded, and missing, has been officially given at about fifteen thousand. There is no official announcement of the Confederate loss, but, in consequence of the superiority of the artillery which the Federals brought into action, it must have exceeded that sustained by the latter.

It is impossible to peruse the narrative of the memorable events which occurred in the vicinity of Richmond during this historic week, without being convinced that General Jackson was in no small degree instrumental in compelling the Federal forces to raise their siege of the city. Before the Confederates commenced their offensive operations, we find his name a tower of strength to them, and a source of continual disquietude to the Federal army. It is easy to observe how the approach of this ubiquitous general was feared by the latter. Rumor followed rumor that he was drawing nigh to the Federal right, each succeeding rumor only tending to intensify the terror which the previous rumors had originated.

At the battle of Gaines's Mill—the only one of the series which can be claimed as a Confederate victory—it is evident that the decisive blow was struck by Jackson when he out-flanked his foes and attacked them so mercilessly on their rear. In the future operations consequent on the Federal retreat, we find him ever active. Placed in prominent com-mand, he harassed the rear of the retreating army until it was considered necessary that the pursuit should be aban-doned. General Lee was well aware of the unsurpassed energy and the unweariness of his companion in arms, and if he gave to him a lion's work, he knew that it would be performed in a manner befitting its importance. It was long before dawn on the first day of the Confederate attack, that Jackson moved from Ashland to take up the position which had been allotted to him ; as day succeeded day in this week of carnage, he was unwearied in his activity ; and it was not until the last shot had been fired in the last battle, that he sheathed his sword and retired from the conflict.

# CHAPTER IX.

## THE CAMPAIGN AGAINST GENERAL POPE.

On the twenty-sixth of June, the National forces, under Generals Fremont, Banks, and McDowell, were consolidated into one army under the name of the Army of Virginia, and General Pope was assigned by the President to the chief command. General Fremont objected to be thus placed in a subordinate command, and at his own request he was relieved from duty, and the corps which he would have commanded in the new army was placed under General Sigel.

It was against this army that General Jackson was called upon to act, after he had reörganized his forces at the close of the battles before Richmond, in which they had suffered

6*

severely, and were considerably lessened in numbers. General Pope was beginning to threaten Richmond from the North, and the new aspect of affairs drew the attention of the Confederates from General McClellan's forces who were resting at Harrison's Landing, preparatory to their evacuation of the Peninsula.

On the eleventh of July, General Halleck was assigned to the command of the whole land forces of the United States, as General-in-Chief.

Shortly after General Pope entering upon his new command, he issued an address to the officers and soldiers of his army which was particularly remarkable for the pretentious language in which it was clothed. He also issued several orders in which he declared that his troops " should subsist upon the country in which their operations are carried on;" and pointed out the manner in which celerity of movement could be best secured by his army. He notified the people of his department that they should be held responsible for any injury done to railroad-trains, bridges, and telegraph-lines, or to any attacks upon trains of straggling soldiers by guerrilla bands; and stated that residents within five miles of any place where any such outrage occurred should be compelled to repair the damage done, or be assessed therefor; and that individuals detected in any outrages against property or persons should be shot without waiting for civil process. He also directed that disloyal male citizens within the lines of his army should be arrested and sent beyond the lines unless they took the oath of allegiance to the United States and gave security for their good behavior; and notified that persons violating such oath would be shot. A retaliatory order issued by the Confederate President, declared that in consequence of General Pope's threatened arrest of disloyal citizens, that general and all commissioned officers serving under him should not be considered as soldiers, and therefore should not be entitled to the benefit of the cartel for the parole of prisoners of war; and that in the event of their being captured they should be held in close confinement as long as General Pope's order should remain in force.

The effective strength of General Pope's army at the commencement of his campaign was thirty-eight thousand infantry and artillery, and about five thousand cavalry. These forces were scattered over a wide district of country not within supporting distance of each other; and General Pope states that he found many of the brigades and divisions badly organized and in a demoralized condition, and that the cavalry was badly mounted and armed, and in poor condition for service. He took an early opportunity not only to reörganize his army, but to concentrate as far as possible all the movable forces under his command; consequently Sigel and Banks's forces were ordered from the valley of the Shenandoah to Sperryville on the east side of the Blue Ridge, and part of McDowell's force to Waterloo Bridge, a point between Warrenton and Sperryville. The remainder of McDowell's corps was left at Falmouth, opposite Fredericksburgh, to cover the crossing of the Rappahannock at that point, and to protect the railroad between it and Acquia

Creek, until the arrival of General Burnside's forces, who were on their way from North-Carolina to Fredericksburgh. These movements were in progress during the time the battles near Richmond were being fought. Their object had been to draw off a portion of the Confederate forces from McClellan's front; but the retreat of the latter commander now enabled General Lee to oppose the greater part of his army to General Pope. General Pope was now called upon to resist at all hazards any advance of the Confederates toward Washington, and to delay and embarrass their movements so as to gain time for the removal of the Army of the Potomac to the banks of the Rappahannock.

In pursuance of this plan, several cavalry expeditions were despatched from Fredericksburgh to destroy the railroad communication between Richmond and the North and the North-west, the latter point leading to the valley of the Shenandoah. These expeditions were completely successful. At the same time General Banks sent all his cavalry and a brigade of infantry on a forced march to Culpeper Court-House, which place was taken possession of, and the cavalry pushed forward to Orange Court-House, where they destroyed the railroad and Confederate stores and munitions of war, and burned the bridge which crossed the Rapidan. After this was accomplished, a force was despatched to Gordonsville with instructions to destroy the railroad east and west of that place, but on the sixteenth of July, before they were enabled to reach it, the town was entered by the advance of Jackson's forces under Ewell, and the proposed movement was thereby rendered impracticable.

General Lee had despatched Jackson with a *corps d'armée* of about twenty-five thousand men to check Pope's advance. This corps consisted of the old Stonewall division, now under the command of General Taliaferro, and the divisions of Ewell and A. P. Hill. Lee then left a small force to watch General McClellan, and proceeded with the main body of his army as rapidly as possible to join General Jackson; but the movement was not accomplished as speedily as was desirable, in consequence of deficiency in the means of transportation. Lee had hoped, with his united forces, to crush Pope's army before McClellan could come to his relief, but a sudden rain-storm so swelled the Rapidan River, rendering it necessary to wait some time before it could be crossed, that the plan was prevented in being carried out, and gave Pope, who took the alarm, time to retire rapidly behind the Rappahannock.

On July the twenty-ninth, General Pope left Washington with his staff for the headquarters of his army in the field. All the preparations having been completed, on the seventh of August he instructed General Banks to move forward from the vicinity of Little Washington to a point midway between Sperryville and Culpeper, McDowell having been ordered on the previous day to advance Rickett's division to Culpeper Court-House. He had thus on that day twenty-eight thousand infantry and artillery assembled along the turnpike from Sperryville to Culpeper. Sigel's corps was stationed at Sperryville, Buford's cavalry at Madison Court-House, and Bayard's cavalry near Rapidan Station, the point where the Orange and Alexandia Railroad crosses the Rapidan River. On the eighth, General Bayard was compelled to fall back slowly from his advanced position on the Rapidan, in the direction of Culpeper Court-House, in consequence of the advance of Jackson's forces, who were reported to be marching not only upon Culpeper, but on Madison Court-House.

In consequence of these movements of the Rebels, General Pope considered it advisable to concentrate his entire force near Culpeper, and to push forward Crawford's brigade of Banks's corps in the direction of Cedar Mountain,* as a support to General Bayard, who was falling back in that direction. At the same time a force was so placed that, if necessary, it could protect Madison Court-House.

Owing to a misunderstanding of the order he received, General Sigel did not arrive at Culpeper Court-House until several hours after the time that he should have reached that point. Consequently, on the morning of the ninth, General Pope was compelled to direct Banks to move forward to Cedar Mountain with his whole corps, and there join Crawford's brigade, instead of ordering Sigel's corps to the front, as he had intended.

General Jackson moved forward from Gordonsville shortly before dawn on the morning of Friday, the eighth. About

---

* This mountain, which is a "sugar-loaf" eminence, is sometimes called Slaughter Mountain, it being the property of the Rev. D. F. Slaughter.

noon his cavalry came into contact with those of General
Bayard, and after a short engagement drove them back.
The Confederate troops encamped for the night at a place
called Garnett's Farm.   Early on the morning of the ninth,
they again took up their line of march, and during the
morning found the Federal cavalry drawn up in line of
battle to receive them.   After waiting some time to find
out their intentions, General Ewell ordered his artillery to
fire upon them, which had the effect of compelling them to
seek the cover of the woods.   Jackson's infantry then advanced, and during the afternoon his force took up a strong
position upon the side of Cedar Mountain.

In the mean time, General Banks's corps moved steadily
forward, under a blazing sun and over dusty roads which
led toward the mountain.   Four or five miles south of
Culpeper this mountain was seen rising directly in front
of the advancing army, although it was still about five
miles distant.   The road led almost up to the left of the
mountain, and then took a sudden curve and wound around
to its right.   General Banks formed his troops in line of
battle in an open meadow lying between the mountain and
the road.   This was accomplished at half-past four P.M.,
when General Banks sent word to his superior officer that
he hardly expected an engagement to take place that day.
His courier had, however, but just started when firing was
heard upon the left of his line, and in a few moments a
perfect stream of flame belched forth from the mountain,
extending from the extreme left to the right wing.   The

engagement commenced about five o'clock, and the firing did not finally terminate until past midnight.

On Jackson's side a part of Ewell's division led in the attack, and was afterward reënforced by a portion of A. P. Hill's division, the whole numbering about fifteen thousand. Banks's corps, which comprised the entire of the Federal force brought into action, did not number more than eight thousand. Early in the battle, Ewell's troops were in danger of being flanked, and were compelled to fall back, disputing every inch of ground and losing a number of prisoners. They were, however, immediately reënforced, when a most desperate hand-to-hand encounter took place. Jackson's troops charged upon the Federals with great valor, and were bravely met. Bayonets locked and sabres crossed, and each man fought as if the fortunes of the field depended on himself alone. And when the bayonet failed to do its work, or was broken or lost, the contest was continued with clubbed guns, until the Federals were compelled to seek refuge in flight. Here the loss on both sides was terrible, and here fell some of the best and bravest officers of the Southern army. But their comrades pressed forward over their dead bodies, and finally gained a complete but a dear-bought victory, in which they not only released their companions who had been captured in the early part of the fight, but captured a number of the Federals in return.

The losses which many of the Federal regiments sustained in this engagement were extremely severe, some of them retiring from the field of battle with barely half their numbers, whilst others, at the termination of the encounter, had almost ceased to have an existence. The manner in which General Banks handled the small force at his command is worthy of the highest commendation. There can be little doubt but that had he been properly supported, and promptly reünforced by even a portion of the large number of troops who were within a short distance of the battle-field, the tide of victory would have been turned. There was evidently great culpability in some quarter, but it is difficult to define on whose shoulders the blame must rest. The division of General Ricketts remained three hours within sound of the battle, but did not move an inch; not, however, because that General did not desire to take part in the engagement, but because he was under the curb of a superior officer, and that officer still awaiting the orders of his superior. General Ricketts, as well as other Generals within call, would gladly have been in the thickest of the fight, but having been officers in the regular army they were too much accustomed to its regular discipline to march to the relief of General Banks without orders. General Pope eventually led Ricketts's division to Banks's assistance, and also pushed Sigel's corps, which had begun to arrive, to the front, but when these movements took place the evening was so far advanced that they failed to regain the ground which had been lost and to change the fortunes of the day.

During the engagement, General Banks had a narrow escape with his life, from a shell which exploded in the midst of his body-guard and killed six of them. Generals Pope and McDowell had also at a later period an equally narrow escape of being either killed or captured. Shortly after midnight they had dismounted in the front to rest a few minutes from the saddle, when Jackson's cavalry made so sudden a dash upon them that they had barely time to mount and ride rapidly away. In so doing they were mistaken by a company of their own men for charging rebel cavalry, and received their fire, which fortunately only killed some of their horses.

General Jackson's official report of the battle of Cedar Mountain is here given, as it illustrates the character of the man. It is remarkable for its brevity. He had invariably little to say in reference to his own achievements, and preferred to be judged by his actions rather than by his words.

HEADQUARTERS VALLEY DISTRICT, }<br>
August 12—6½ P.M. }

COLONEL: On the evening of the ninth instant, God blessed our arms with another victory. The battle was near Cedar Run, about six miles from Culpeper Court-House. The enemy, according to the statement of prisoners, consisted of Banks's, McDowell's, and Sigel's commands. We have over four hundred prisoners, including Brig.-General Prince. While our list of killed is less than that of the enemy, yet we have to mourn the loss of some of our best officers and men. Brig.-General Charles S. Winder was mortally wounded while ably discharging his duty at the head of his command, which was the advance of the left wing of the army. We have collected about one thousand five hundred small arms, and other ordnance-stores.

I am, Colonel, your obedient servant,

T. J. JACKSON, Major-General.

Col. R. H. CHILTON, A.A.G.

The Federal loss in the battle was about one thousand eight hundred in killed, wounded, and prisoners, besides which fully one thousand men straggled back to Culpeper Court-House and beyond, and never entirely returned to their commands. The Confederates, according to their own reports, did not suffer a loss of much over seven hundred in killed and wounded. The advantageous position which the latter occupied during the battle naturally sheltered them from the Federal fire.

At daybreak on the morning of the tenth, Jackson's sharp-shooters were found to occupy the same spot which had been their front at the close of the battle. Several skirmishes and slight engagements took place in the course of the morning, but the battle was not renewed, and in the afternoon Jackson retired from the position which he held. Early on the following morning he retired to the south of the Rapidan, to which river he was followed by a cavalry and artillery force under General Buford. Though Jackson had only fifteen thousand engaged in the action, the entire force he had then under his command, and the remainder of whom came up during the night, was from fifty to sixty thousand.

The seat of war in Virginia was now to revert to the old field of operations in the vicinity of Washington. Not only was General McClellan's army transported, in the middle of August, from the James River to Alexandria and Acquia Creek on the banks of the Potomac, but General Burnside had earlier in the month reached Falmouth on the Rappahannock with a considerable force, with which he had been successfully operating in North-Carolina. These changes naturally relieved the main Confederate army from the necessity of closely watching over and protecting the Confederate capital. Consequently, Lee and Longstreet, and other rebel leaders, moved northward to assist Jackson, and Ewell, and Hill, in their proceedings against General Pope. And Gen. Pope, on the other hand, had his army increased by considerable detachments from the commands of McClellan and Burnside.

After the battle of Cedar Mountain, Jackson fell back to the south of the Rapidan, with the view of moving westward and outflanking Pope on his right; whilst he resigned the front to Generals Lee and Longstreet, who were rapidly approaching from Richmond. Pope being reënforced by a portion of Burnside's forces under General Reno, again moved forward to the Rapidan, and took up a strong position on that river. He, however, became convinced by the eighteenth of August that he was about to be confronted by the main Confederate army, and feared that he might be attacked by overwhelming numbers before he could be reënforced by any portion of the army of the Potomac. He therefore retired from the line of the Rapidan, and fell back to the Rappahannock, the entire army safely crossing the latter river on the eighteenth and nineteenth. The troops of Jackson, followed by those of Lee and Longstreet, advanced in close proximity to the Federals, as the latter retired. On the twentieth, and two following days, the Rebels made efforts to cross the river at various points, but were unable to effect their purpose from the rapid and continuous artillery fire with which they were opposed.  The Rebels now moved slowly up the river for the purpose of turning Pope's right, whilst the latter being required to keep himself in communication with Fredericksburgh, was unable to extend his lines farther westward.  During the night of the twenty-second, a dashing raid was made by a large force of Stuart's cavalry upon Catlett's Station, in the rear of the Federal army.  They captured General Pope's private baggage, letters, official papers, and plans of his campaign, along with several prisoners, attacked a railroad train, and destroyed a number of army wagons filled with supplies.

General Pope determined on the twenty-second that on the following day he would recross the river, near Rappahannock Station, and fall furiously with his whole force upon the flank and rear of Lee's army, then moving toward his right.  A heavy storm occurring that night, carried away all the bridges, and destroyed all the fords, and thus rendered the proposed attack impracticable.

The Confederate forces who at this time confronted General Pope on the Rappahannock, were those of Lee and Longstreet.  To Jackson had been assigned another duty, and it was one for which he was especially fitted, from the rapidity with which he was ever able to move large masses of troops between distant points.  The task which had been allotted to him was to move to the west of the Bull Run Mountains, and then crossing that range at Thoroughfare

Gap, march upon the rear of the Federal right, and fall upon their flank.   Let us follow Jackson in this detour.

On the evening of the twenty-second, he bivouacked opposite Sulphur Springs, and threw over the river two brigades of Ewell's division.   These brigades met with opposition from the Federals, and were withdrawn on the following night, after some sharp fighting.

On Monday morning, the twenty-fifth, Jackson was confronted at the same place by a heavy Federal force, and some firing took place, but without much loss having been sustained therefrom.   That evening Jackson's whole force moved up to Jefferson, in Culpeper County, whence it marched through Amosville, in Rappahannock County, and then still farther up the river.   The Federals appeared to have been unaware of this movement, as Longstreet remained for some time on the Rappahannock, in the neighborhood of Sulphur Springs, and covered the commencement of Jackson's march.   The latter crossed the river within ten miles of the Blue Ridge, and then marched across open fields, by strange country paths and comfortable homesteads, passed the little town of Orleans, and reached Salem, on the Manassas Gap Railroad, about midnight.   By day-dawn of Tuesday, his troops were again on the march, and proceeded along the Manassas Gap road to Thoroughfare Gap, in the Bull Run Mountains; thence to Gainesville, and on to Bristow Station, on the Orange and Alexandria Railroad, four miles south of Manassas Junction; thus accomplishing the march from Amosville, of about forty-eight miles, in the same number of hours.  At Bristow he captured a railroad train and several prisoners, and tore up the track.

On the twenty-seventh, Jackson moved up to Manassas Junction, where he found an immense amount of stores of every description, to which his troops freely helped themselves.  "It was a curious sight," writes one of his soldiers, "to see our ragged and famished men helping themselves to every imaginable article of luxury or necessity, whether of clothing, food, or what not.  For my part, I got a tooth-brush, a box of candles, a quantity of lobster-salad, a barrel of coffee, and other things which I forget. . . . Our men had been living on roasted corn since crossing the Rappahannock, and we had brought no wagons, so we could carry little away of the riches before us.  But the men could eat, for one meal at least.  So they were marched up, and as much of every thing eatable served out as they could carry.  To see a starving man eating lobster-salad and drinking Rhine wine, bare-footed and in tatters, was curious; the whole thing was incredible."

Jackson's situation was certainly now a very critical one, for he had placed himself and his eighteen thousand jaded men, who here comprised the entire number of his corps, between Alexandria and Warrenton—between the forces of McClellan at the former place and those of Pope at the latter.

When General Pope learned that Jackson was approaching his rear by Thoroughfare Gap, he felt satisfied, from the promise of reënforcements which he had received, that he would be in a position to give battle to and defeat him before he could be joined by Longstreet, who was also making his way by the same route.  General Pope assigned to his corps commanders certain positions which they should occupy to enable him to carry out his plan.  The non-arrival of the reënforcements at the time promised, seriously interfered with the Federal General's arrangements, and the non-compliance of certain of his corps commanders with his instructions, completely frustrated his plans, and enabled Jackson to reach Manassas without encountering any serious obstacle, beyond an engagement which took place between Ewell's division and that of General Hooker, at Kettle Run, upon the approach of the former toward Bristow Station.

Jackson being now separated from the main body of the Rebel army, General Pope was naturally anxious to prevent any junction of Longstreet's forces with his, and for this purpose he despatched Generals McDowell, Kearny, and Reno, to Gainesville and Greenwich, east of Thoroughfare Gap.  These officers reached those points on the night of the twenty-seventh, and completely cut off Jackson from the main body of the Rebel army, that was still west of the Bull Run range.  To enable General Pope to more thoroughly cover Washington, he found it necessary to break off his communication with Fredericksburgh, so that he could mass his forces in greater numbers in the district where danger was most imminent.

We have stated that General Jackson had placed himself

in a critical position, but if he had been aware of the weakness of the Federal line to the south of Manassas Junction, owing to the non-compliance of General Porter with orders received from his commanding general, he might have inflicted a severe blow on the Federals in that quarter. General Pope, in his report, thus explains the position : "There were but two courses left open to Jackson, in consequence of this sudden and unexpected movement of the army. He could not retrace his steps through Gainesville, as it was occupied by McDowell, having at command a force equal, if not superior, to his own. He was either obliged, therefore, to retreat through Centreville, which would carry him still farther from the main body of Lee's army, or to mass his force, assault us at Bristow Station, and turn our right. He pursued the former course, and retired through Centreville. This mistake of Jackson's alone saved us from the serious consequences which would have followed this disobedience of orders on the part of General Porter."

During the early part of the night of the twenty-seventh, General Pope being satisfied of Jackson's position, sent orders to McDowell, Kearny, and Reno, to advance from Gainesville and Greenwich to Manassas Junction and Bristow. Kearny reached Bristow at eight o'clock the following morning, and was immediately pushed forward in pursuit of Jackson toward Manassas, followed by Hooker. Reno was at the time on the left, marching direct upon the Junction, but McDowell being delayed in his movement from Gainesville, enabled Jackson to retreat toward Cen-

7

treville, a performance which he hardly would have been able to accomplish, had McDowell arrived in time to intercept his crossing at Bull Run.

At night-fall on the twenty-seventh, Jackson set fire to the dépôt, store-houses, loaded trains, and other Government property at Manassas Junction, and as the conflagration had begun to subside, the Stonewall, or First division of his corps, moved off toward the battle-field of Manassas, and the other two divisions to Centreville, six miles distant. General Pope reached Manassas Junction, with Kearny's and Reno's troops, about mid-day of the twenty-eighth, less than an hour after Jackson in person had retired. These forces, along with those of Hooker, were sent in pursuit, and orders were forwarded to McDowell to change his march to the direction of Centreville. Late in the day, Jackson's rear-guard was driven out of Centreville, and the place occupied by Kearny. One part of Jackson's force now moved by Sudley Springs, and the other pursued the turnpike road toward Gainesville. King's division of McDowell's corps encountered the advance of Jackson's force about six o'clock in the evening, as it was making for Thoroughfare Gap. A severe action took place, which terminated at dark, each party maintaining his ground. Jackson had returned to within six miles of the Gap through which Longstreet must come, and whose arrival he anxiously longed for. General Pope now so arranged his forces that he felt satisfied there was no room left for Jackson's escape. McDowell, Sigel, and Reynolds, with twenty-five thousand men, were to the west, situated between him and his reënforcements; whilst twenty-five thousand more, under Kearny and other generals, approached him from the opposite side. With these forces, General Pope felt satisfied that he could crush Jackson before the latter could receive any aid from Longstreet. Unfortunately, however, General King, from some misapprehension, fell back to Manassas Junction, and left open the line of communication between the Rebel forces, which rendered new combinations of troops necessary on the part of the Federal commander.

The Federal plan now consisted in massing the entire force upon Jackson, and compelling him to fight. General Sigel commenced the attack about daylight on the morning of the twenty-ninth, a mile or two east of Groveton, near Bull Run, where he was soon joined by the divisions of Hooker and Kearny. Jackson fell back several miles, but was so closely pressed by these forces that he was compelled to make a stand and to offer the best defence possible. He accordingly took up a position with his left in the neighborhood of Sudley Springs, his right a little to the south of Warrenton turnpike, and his line covered by an old railroad grade which leads from Gainesville in the direction of Leesburgh. His batteries, which were numerous, and some of them of heavy calibre, were posted behind the ridges in the open ground on both sides of Warrenton turnpike, while the mass of his troops were sheltered in dense woods behind the railroad embankments.

The battle continued without intermission until mid-day, when both armies were considerably cut up from the sharp action in which they had been engaged. From twelve until four o'clock, severe skirmishing occurred constantly at various points of the line.

Heintzelman and Reno recommenced the attack about half-past five, as at that time information was received that McDowell was advancing to join the main body of the Federal army, and Porter should at the same time have been ready to have entered into action, if he had obeyed the peremptory order given him. By this attack, the whole of Jackson's left was doubled back toward his centre, and the National troops, after a sharp conflict for an hour and a half, occupied the field of battle, with Jackson's dead and wounded in their hands. McDowell now arriving on the field, was immediately pushed to the front, along the Warrenton turnpike, with orders to fall upon Jackson, who was retreating toward the turnpike from the direction of Sudley Springs. This attack was made by King's division, about sunset; but by that time the advance of the main body of the Confederate army, under Longstreet, had begun to reach the field, and King encountered a stubborn and determined resistance at a point three quarters of a mile in front of the Federal line of battle. In the mean time, Heintzelman and Reno continued to push back Jackson's left in the direction of the turnpike, so that about eight o'clock they occupied the greater portion of the field of battle. Porter took no part in the action, but suffered his troops to lie idle on their arms, within sight and sound of the conflict during the entire day. General Pope is of opinion that had he received Porter's assistance before the arrival of Longstreet, the larger portion of Jackson's force would have been utterly crushed or captured before sufficient reënforcements could have been received by him wherewith to make an effective resistance possible. The losses this day were extremely heavy on both sides.

During the night of the twenty-ninth, and up to ten o'clock on the morning of the thirtieth, there were numerous indications that the Confederates were retreating from the Federal front, and reconnoissances ascertained that they were retiring in the direction of Gainesville. The National troops were so exhausted from long fasting and hard fighting that their commander considered it indispensable that they should be reënforced; but the required reënforcements not being forthcoming, he determined that he would again give battle to the Rebels, and, if possible, so cripple them that they could make no farther advance toward the National capital. The force which General Pope had available for action upon this day was about forty thousand men, which number included seven thousand of Porter's corps. The remainder (five thousand) of the latter, had been marched off at daylight to Centreville, and were thus rendered unavailable for operations on that day. Banks's corps was at Bristow Station, guarding the railroad and wagon trains of the army.

The point at which our narrative now arrives is the commencement of the second battle of Bull Run, which took place close to the far-famed battle-field of that name. The Confederates were posted with Longstreet on the right, and Jackson on the left, and formed an obtuse angle. It was presumed by this arrangement that if the Federals forced either of the Confederate Generals back, their flank would be exposed to the direct attack of the other. The Federal left rested upon that portion of the Bull-Run battle-field, which on the previous year was occupied by the main body of the Rebel army. The line extended in the direction of Manassas Junction. Though there were skirmishing and some slight cannonading during the morning, the battle did not begin until about one o'clock.

The Federals made the attack. General Pope found it necessary to act promptly, as Jackson was continuing to be rapidly reënforced by the main Rebel army, portions of which had been arriving during the whole of the previous night and throughout that morning. Pope was already confronted by greatly superior forces, and these forces were every moment being largely increased by fresh arrivals.

Porter's corps and King's division were moved forward to the attack upon the turnpike, and Heintzelman and Reno were pushed to the right to attack Jackson's left in flank. The Confederates massed their troops as fast as they arrived on the field on their right, and quickly moved forward from that direction to turn the Federal left. Ricketts's division was immediately posted so that it could resist this movement. Porter's troops soon retired in considerable confusion, having made neither a vigorous nor persistent attack. This retrograde movement led the Rebels to advance to the assault, and the whole Federal line was soon furiously engaged. The main attack was on the left, but it was stubbornly resisted by Schenck, Milroy, Reynolds, and Ricketts. The battle raged furiously for several hours, the Confederates bringing up their heavy reserves, pouring mass after mass of troops upon the Federal left, and while overpowering it, assaulting the right with superior forces. Porter's troops were again sent into action on the left, where they rendered distinguished service, especially the brigade of regulars under Colonel Buchanan; but notwithstanding the utmost firmness and obstinacy of the National forces, the odds were too great for successful resistance, and they were ultimately compelled to retire.

At sunset the wings of the Confederate army swept round in pursuit—Jackson swinging his left on the right as a pivot, and Longstreet swinging his right on his left. But the Federals were enabled to retire in perfect order. Night closed the contest, and put a stop to the slaughter, which, as in the battle of the previous day, had been great in the extreme.

General Pope felt that he was no longer able to maintain his position so far to the front against such overwhelming numbers, and with such weakened and fatigued forces as those he commanded. He therefore determined to retire to Centreville, and the movement was made without any difficulty and without any pursuit being attempted by the

Rebels. General Banks was also ordered to retire from Bristow to Centreville, and to destroy such trains and stores as he could not carry with him.

The thirty-first of August was comparatively a quiet day. On the following morning, the Confederates moved heavy columns toward the Federal right, in the direction of Fairfax Court-House. In consequence of the great exhaustion of his men, General Pope desired to delay an engagement until the following day, but the Rebel movement became so developed by the afternoon of September the first, that it was evident it was made with a view of turning the Federal right, and cutting off the line of communications with Washington. This had to be resisted at all hazards. The necessary dispositions of troops were made to stop the Rebel progress, and a very severe action occurred at Chantilly, a place north of Centreville, and north-west of Fairfax Court-House, and about six miles distant from each. The engagement took place in the midst of a terrific thunder-storm. It was not terminated until after dark, when the Confederates were entirely driven back from the Federal front. This battle was especially unfortunate to the North, as it deprived it of the life of General Kearny, whose services on many fields had rendered his name distinguished.

The engagement at Chantilly closed the Confederate campaign against General Pope. It will be observed that throughout it General Jackson was given the most prominent place. The campaign was commenced by him alone; and after he was joined by Lee and Longstreet, we find him invariably pushed forward as the pioneer during the remainder of its progress. The battle of Cedar Mountain was fought by him alone. In the battle of Groveton he had, unaided, to contend against a much superior force, and if it had not been for difficulties in the Federal camp, already alluded to, there can be little doubt but that he would there have suffered a severe defeat. In the closing actions of the campaign he was joined by the main body of the Confederate army, and though the honor of the victory could not in them be entirely awarded to him, it is evident that no inconsiderable share thereof can be claimed on his behalf.

7

# CHAPTER X.

## THE INVASION OF MARYLAND.

The Federals retire within the Lines of Washington—Resignation of Pope
—Appointment of McClellan—Jackson leads the Way into Maryland—
Enters Frederick—Incidents during its Occupation—Lee's Proclamation
—Jackson marches upon Harper's Ferry—Maryland Heights abandoned
—Harper's Ferry bombarded—Its Surrender—Jackson's Report of the
Capture—Federal Inquiry into the Cause of Surrender—Battle of South-
Mountain—Battle of Antietam—The Battle-ground and Positions of the
Combatants—Terrific Contest between Jackson and Hooker—Change in
the Scene of Conflict—The Losses—Jackson demolishes Thirty Miles of
Railroad—Affair at Blackford's Ford.

AFTER the battle of Chantilly, great changes again took
place in the movements of the contending armies, and the
Federal forces on the Potomac were again destined to be
placed under the command of General McClellan.

On the second of September, the remnant of General
Pope's army retired from Centreville, and moved within the
lines of Washington, but not without suffering early on the
morning of that day the loss of one hundred wagons filled
with commissary stores, which were captured by the Rebels
between Centreville and Fairfax Court-House, at that time
the rear of the Federal army. On the same day General
Pope desired to be relieved from his command. His resig-

nation was accepted by the President, and General McClellan was at once appointed to the "command of the fortifications at Washington, and of all the troops for the defence of the capital."

The events of the past week rendered it advisable to concentrate the National forces as much as possible. Consequently, on the day after the second battle of Bull Run, General Burnside removed his stores from Fredericksburgh, evacuated the place, destroyed the bridges crossing the river, and retired with his forces to Acquia Creek, where he placed himself under the protection of the gunboats. Two days later, the Federal forces under General Julius White evacuated Winchester, and retired to Harper's Ferry.

Every preparation was made to resist a direct attack should it be made upon Washington by the Confederates, which it was naturally feared would result from the defeat of the Federal forces in front. The various garrisons were strengthened and put in order, and the troops were so disposed that they covered all the approaches to the city, and could be readily thrown upon threatened points. But it was no part of the plan of the Confederate General to hurl his forces against fortifications. He rather preferred to initiate a new era in the history of the war. The Confederate theory had thus far been that in battling against the Northern soldiers, who had marched in measured tread over Southern soil, they were acting strictly on the defensive, and merely desired to expel the "invader" from their land. This assumed defensive action was now to be changed into one of offence, and for the first time during the Rebellion a Confederate army was to plant its standard over Northern soil.

It was anticipated that if a strong Confederate force was present in Maryland, there would be found in that State "an uprising of the people" in favor of the South, which would result in the secession of that State, and the severance of Washington from the loyal North.

The Confederates, having driven the Federal army under cover of the guns which bristled on the hill-tops around Washington, had no desire to spend their time in inactivity, and the smoke which curled upward from the last hostile gun was scarcely more rapidly cleared away from the sky than were the numerous troops under the command of Lee and his brother generals removed from the vicinage of the National Capital. Jackson was again the pioneer and moved forward on the march to Maryland on September the third. He passed that night at Drainesville, and on the following day reached Leesburgh, where he was joined by the corps commanded by General D. H. Hill, and other troops. On the fifth the Potomac was crossed by both Jackson's and D. H. Hill's commands in the vicinity of the Point of Rocks, and that day's march continued until past midnight, when the troops bivouacked in the neighborhood of Buckeyestown. At Monocacy Junction, near that place, the telegraph operator, who had failed to receive any notice of the rebel approach, was discovered by General Hill busily occupied in despatching messages on the business of the railroad. The General informed him that he was a prisoner, and desired

him to telegraph in his own name for a large train of cars
to be sent immediately from Baltimore. On the operator
stating that the wires had just been cut, he was desired, as
a test, to despatch information that the Rebels had arrived,
and had taken him prisoner. He repeated his statement,
when one of Hill's men tried the instrument, and found it,
as reported to be, not in working order.

The Rebel troops, after about two or three hours' rest, renewed their march before daybreak, and about ten o'clock
Jackson's advance force entered Frederick, the capital of
Maryland, their music, such as it was, playing "My Maryland" and "Dixie." This advance force consisted of about
five thousand men, and their appearance was of so motley
a nature that it was hardly likely to impress the people of
Frederick in their favor. Their clothes, instead of being
uniform were multiform, and as might naturally be expected
from the rough usage their habiliments had been subject to,
they were neither spotless nor perfect.

The reception was lacking that hearty welcome which
they had calculated upon receiving. Though in some few
instances outrages were committed against property, it must
be admitted that every precaution was taken to prevent
them. Guards were placed at the stores, and only a few
men allowed to enter at a time. They usually paid for
what they took away with such money as they possessed;
but to use the expression of one of the citizens, the "notes
depreciated the paper on which they were printed." It is
true that in some of the most crowded stores, especially

shoe-stores, articles would be smuggled away without payment, but these were exceptional cases. An attack was made by some of the soldiers on the *Examiner* printing-office, and the contents of the office thrown into the street. The Provost-Marshal, however, not only suppressed the riot and put the rioters in the guard-house, but he compelled them to return every thing belonging to the office.

On Sunday, the seventh, all the churches were opened as usual, and General Jackson attended the Presbyterian and German Reformed churches. At the latter place the minister, Dr. Zacharias, prayed for the President of the United States in a firm voice.

Confederate troops continued to arrive in Frederick, and enrollment offices were opened for the purpose of obtaining recruits for the Southern army. On Monday, General Lee issued a proclamation to the people of Maryland, in which he announced to them that he had entered that State for the purpose of restoring her to freedom, and of rescuing her citizens from the thraldom under which they had been placed by Northern bayonets, and giving them an opportunity freely to decide for themselves whether they would join the Southern Confederacy or not.

On Wednesday, the tenth, the Rebel army commenced to move away from Frederick, Jackson, as usual, leading the van. The object which was now to be attained was the capture of Harper's Ferry, with all the Federal forces and munitions of war there situated. It was most important to the Confederates that they should obtain possession of this stronghold. It was the key to the valley of the Shenandoah, and its occupancy would not only enable them to obtain their supplies by that direction, but it would open to them a road for retreat in the event of a retrograde movement becoming necessary.

It was considered advisable that the place should be approached and attacked from various points. General Walker's division proceeded by the Point of Rocks (destroying on its way the canal aqueduct at the mouth of the Monocacy) to Loudon Heights, separated from Harper's Ferry by the Shenandoah River. At the same time, the divisions of General McLaws and R. H. Anderson moved for Maryland Heights, which overlooked the place from the northern side of the Potomac. Whilst these Generals were marching to their respective positions, General Jackson made a detour for the purpose of attacking the stronghold from the south-west. He re-crossed the Potomac at Williamsport, and then marched upon Martinsburgh, twenty miles above Harper's Ferry. Upon his approach, three or four thousand Federal soldiers who were stationed at the last-named place, fell back and united with the forces at Harper's Ferry. Jackson pursued them, and on the morning of Saturday, the thirteenth, reached Halltown, four miles south-west of the Ferry. From this point he communicated with General Walker, who was already in possession of Loudon Heights, and with Generals McLaws and Anderson, to whom the heights on the Maryland side had been most unaccountably surrendered by the Federal officer in command, and directed them to open fire on the following (Sunday) morning, by which time he would have his guns in position. Maryland Heights had been attacked on that morning, and the position had been stoutly defended, but, about four o'clock in the afternoon, the Federal regiments retreated down the mountain in good order, having first spiked their guns, and then crossed the river to Harper's Ferry. No sooner had they retired than the Confederates occupied the heights above the guns, and deliberately commenced a musketry-fire upon the village below. However, a shell from one of the Federal batteries posted near the bridge soon dislodged them from this position. Colonel Ford, who commanded the Heights, was afterwards dismissed the Federal service for military incapacity and abandoning this position without sufficient cause.

Every thing was quiet within Harper's Ferry on Sunday morning. There was no enemy in sight, with the exception of Jackson's forces, who were in front. Every person expected to be awakened with the booming of artillery from the evacuated Heights, and the silence which reigned was not ominous of good. About noon, two companies of the Garibaldi Guard bravely ascended the Maryland Heights and secured some of their camp equipage, and brought down four of the pieces of artillery which had been left spiked the previous day. Hour after hour passed by, and no signs of the Rebels appearing on the heights, it began to be imagined that they had been foiled in their plans, and that the only force to contend with would be that in front.

Preparations, however, had been made to resist any assault, although it was evident that resistance would be useless, unless reenforcements could be received.

About two o'clock in the afternoon, the silence was broken by a furious fire which burst forth simultaneously on every side. Shot and shell flew in every direction, and the soldiers and citizens were compelled to seek refuge behind rocks and houses, and in every nook and corner which offered a friendly shelter against the unwelcome visitors. The Federal artillery replied with much spirit. Heavy cannonading was brought to bear upon them from five different points, yet they held their own manfully. However, before night closed the struggle, they had been compelled to contract their lines, and Jackson's forces occupied some intrenchments which the Federals had been compelled to desert on the hills of Bolivar. That night General Jackson sent a message to General Walker that his forces were in possession of the first line of the Federal intrenchments, and that, with God's blessing, he would have Harper's Ferry and the National forces early the next morning.

The fight was renewed the following (Monday) morning at five o'clock. The attack was obstinately resisted until about eight o'clock, when the ammunition of the Federals gave out, and it was deemed impossible for them to hold out any longer. A council of war was immediately held, when it was decided, but not unanimously, that the place should be surrendered. White flags were run up in every direction, and a flag of truce was sent to inquire on what

162     LIFE OF GEN. T. J. JACKSON.

conditions a surrender would be accepted. General Jackson demanded an unconditional surrender; but he eventually agreed that the officers should be allowed to go out with their side arms and private effects and the rank and file with every thing except arms and equipments.

A murmur of disapprobation ran along the entire Federal line, when it became known that the place had been surrendered. Officers exhibited strong demonstrations of grief, while the soldiers were equally demonstrative in their manifestations of rage.

As soon as the terms of surrender were completed, Generals Jackson and A. P. Hill rode into the town, accompanied by their respective staffs. General Hill immediately selected his headquarters, whilst General Jackson rode down to the river, and then returned to Bolivar Heights, the observed of all observers. He was dressed in the coarsest description of homespun, which bore every mark of having seen much service. An old hat which covered his head harmonized with the rest of his attire—in fact, in his general appearance he was hardly to be distinguished from the rough-looking but hardy fellows who called him their commander.

As soon as Jackson returned from the village the entire Federal force was mustered on Bolivar Heights, preparatory to stacking arms and completing the surrender. All the cavalry, about two thousand, under the command of Colonel Davis, had cut their way out on Sunday night, and had proceeded along the road to Sharpsburgh, capturing an ammunition train, belonging to General Longstreet, and several Rebel prisoners by the way. The number of men, guns, stores, wagons, etc., captured are given in General Jackson's Report, which we here append:

HEADQUARTERS VALLEY DISTRICT, }
September 16, 1862. }

COLONEL: Yesterday God crowned our arms with another brilliant success on the surrender at Harper's Ferry of Brigadier-General White and eleven thousand troops, an equal number of small arms, seventy-three pieces of artillery, and about two hundred wagons. In addition to other stores, there is a large amount of camp and garrison equipage. Our loss was very small. The meritorious conduct of both officers and men will be mentioned in a more extended report.

I am, Colonel, your obedient servant,

T. J. JACKSON, Major-General.

Colonel R. H. CHILTON, Assistant Adjutant-General.

The officer in command of Harper's Ferry, at the time of its surrender, was Colonel D. S. Miles, and the surrender was the subject of a court of inquiry. General Julius White, who was present at the time, had merely taken refuge there on the retirement of his forces from Winchester and Martinsburgh. Throughout the attack he acted with decided capability and courage, and on Sunday led his troops against Jackson on Bolivar Heights. During the siege he assumed a subordinate position, and at the close of the engagement he was sent by Colonel Miles to arrange terms for a surrender. The Confederates did not cease firing for more than half an hour after the white flag had been raised, during which time Colonel Miles was mortally wounded.

The court of inquiry, in pronouncing judgment upon Colonel Miles in reference to this surrender, says: "An officer who cannot appear before any earthly tribunal to answer or explain charges gravely affecting his character, who has met his death at the hands of the enemy, even upon the spot he disgracefully surrenders, is entitled to the tenderest care and most careful investigation. This the commission has accorded Colonel Miles, and, in giving a decision, only repeats what runs through over nine hundred pages of testimony, entirely unanimous upon the fact that Colonel Miles's incapacity, amounting almost to imbecility, led to the shameful surrender of this important post." Re-enforcements were but a few miles distant at the time of the surrender, but the Court was of opinion that sufficient alacrity had not been displayed in forwarding them to the relief of the beleaguered place. It remarked *inter alia:* "Had the garrison been slower to surrender, or the army of the Potomac swifter to march, the enemy would have been forced to raise the siege, or would have been taken in detail, with the Potomac dividing his force."

During the occurrence of the events which we have thus far narrated in this chapter, there was great activity in the Federal camp. The disappearance of Lee's army from the front at Washington, and its passage into Maryland, enlarged the sphere of McClellan's operations, and made an active campaign necessary to cover Baltimore, prevent the invasion of Pennsylvania, and drive the Rebels out of Maryland.

The advance of the Federal army under General Burnside entered Frederick on September the twelfth. While at Frederick, on the following day, General McClellan considered it was necessary to force the passage of the South-Mountain range, and by that route afford relief to Harper's Ferry, the siege of which he had been already made acquainted with. The two armies came into collision at Crampton's and Turner's Passes, on the South-Mountain range, on Sunday, the day upon which the bombardment of Harper's Ferry was commenced. The action resulted in the two Passes being carried, and in important military positions being gained by the Federal army.

On the day after this engagement General Lee's army fell back toward Antietam Creek, situated from six to eight miles west of the South-Mountain range, and running for some distance almost parallel thereto. This creek, from which the battle we are now about to chronicle derives its name, rises in Central Pennsylvania, and after running in a southerly direction, mingles its waters with those of the Potomac, about five miles above Harper's Ferry. This battle is called by the Confederates Sharpsburgh, such being the name of the town in the vicinity of which it was fought. In this new position Lee was enabled to resist any attack upon him, and to cover the Shepherdstown Ford on the

Potomac, by which he would be enabled to form a junction with Jackson at Harper's Ferry.

On the fifteenth McClellan pushed his army forward to Antietam Creek, in the hopes of coming up with Lee during the day in sufficient force to beat him again and drive him into the river. But the day was too far advanced before he had an opportunity of making an attack. On the following morning he found that the Confederates had slightly changed their line, and were posted on the heights near Antietam Creek.

Before the prisoners taken by Jackson at Harper's Ferry could be paroled, that General found it necessary to leave suddenly with twenty thousand troops for the reënforcement of Lee, leaving A. P. Hill with his division in command of the captured city. General Ewell having been severely wounded at the battle of Groveton, and amputation of the leg rendered necessary, his division was commanded by General Lawton. The Stonewall division was commanded by General Stark, its previous chief, General Taliaferro, having also been severely wounded in the same battle.

Let us describe the field upon which the approaching battle was to be fought, and the positions of the combatants at the commencement of the struggle.

The Confederate line was drawn up upon the right or western bank of Antietam Creek, upon a small peninsula formed by the waters of that creek and the Potomac, which river is the western and southern boundary. Their left and centre were upon and in front of the road from Sharpsburgh to Hagerstown, and were protected by woods and irregularities of the ground. Their extreme left rested upon a wooded eminence near the cross-roads to the north of Miller's farm, the distance at this point between the road and the Potomac, which makes here a great bend to the east, being about three fourths of a mile. Their right rested on the hills to the right of Sharpsburgh, near Snavely's farm, covering the crossing of the Antietam and the approaches to the town from the south-east. The ground from their immediate front to the Antietam is undulating. Hills intervene, whose crests in general are commanded by the crests of others in their rear. The position was favorably located for both offensive and defensive operations, and occupied a range of hills forming a semi-circle, with the concave toward the National army. The arrangement of the line was as follows: General Jackson on the extreme left, General Longstreet in the centre, and General D. H. Hill on the extreme right.

The Federals occupied a position on the opposite or eastern bank of Antietam Creek, in close proximity to the road leading from Boonsboro to Sharpsburgh, having the creek in front, and the Elk Mountain range in their rear. The position was much less commanding than that held by the Confederates; the extreme right, however, rested upon a height commanding the extreme Confederate left. The forces on the extreme right were commanded by General Hooker, (supported by General Mansfield,) and those on the extreme left by General Burnside. The centre was occupied by the corps of Generals Sumner, Franklin, and Fitz-John Porter whose forces were held in reserve, so that, if necessary, they could render assistance to either the right or left wing, on whichever the force of battle might fall. Unsupported, attack in front was impossible. McClellan's forces lay behind low, disconnected ridges, in front of the Rebel summits, all or nearly all being 'unwooded. They gave, however, some sover for artillery, and guns were therefore massed on the centre. The lines stretched four miles from right to left.

It will thus be seen that Jackson and Hooker were placed in antagonistic positions to each other at one end of the lines, and Burnside and D. H. Hill confronted each other at the other end. In the centre, Longstreet faced Sumner, Franklin, and Porter.

The numbers of the men actually brought into action with each other were about one hundred thousand in each army, and one hundred guns on each side belched forth their deadly missiles.

The battle commenced on the afternoon of the sixteenth by Hooker's corps, consisting of Ricketts's and Doubleday's divisions, and the Pennsylvania reserves, under General Meade. They were sent across the creek by a ford and bridge to the right of Kedysville, with orders to attack, and if possible to turn the Rebel left. General Mansfield's corps was sent in the evening to support Hooker. Placed in position, Meade's division, the Pennsylvania reserves, which was at the head of Hooker's corps, became engaged in a sharp contest with the enemy, which lasted until after dark, at which time it had succeeded in driving in a portion of the opposing line, and held the ground.

The sun of September the seventeenth rose upon a bright, but a blood-stained day. With its earliest light, the contest was opened between Hooker and Jackson. Between six and seven o'clock the Federals advanced a large body of skirmishers, and shortly after the main body of Hooker's corps was hurled against the division of General Lawton. When we consider that Jackson and Hooker were the two Generals who in this portion of the battle-field were pitted against each other, it is almost useless to say that the contest was severe, and that the fortunes of the day were varying. Now an advance, and then a repulse. Then again another advance, to be followed by another repulse. Words like these, with the addition of phrases referring to the receipt of reënforcements, are almost sufficient with which to write the history of this encounter. If one was for a time driven back, it was but for a time. With increased energy, he not only gained his lost ground, but drove back his foe in return.

Hooker's attack was successful for a time, but masses of Rebels having been thrown upon him, his progress was checked. So severe was the clash of arms at one time, that upon his troops closing up their shattered lines, there was a regiment where a brigade had been, and hardly a brigade where a whole division had been victorious. When Mans-

8

field brought up his corps to Hooker's support, the two corps drove the Confederates back—the gallant and distinguished veteran Mansfield losing his life in the effort. About the same time, General Hooker was wounded and had to leave the field. The command devolved on Sumner, whose corps had come up to the Federal relief. The firing was now fearful and incessant. At one period when the Federals had obtained a position which enabled them to pour a flanking fire upon their foes, General Stark, who commanded the Stonewall division, galloped to the front of his brigade, and seizing the standard, rallied his men. This gallant act cost him his life, for, as he threw himself in the van, four bullets pierced his body, and he fell dead upon the field. The effect, instead of discouraging the soldiers, fired them with determination and revenge, and caused them to dash forward, drive back the Federals, and regain a position which they kept during the rest of the day.

Two divisions of Franklin's corps were, during the afternoon, added to the strength of the Federal right, where the condition of things was not particularly promising, notwithstanding the success which had been wrested from the Rebels by the stubborn bravery of the troops. Sumner's, Hooker's, and Mansfield's corps had lost heavily, and several general officers had been carried from the field. Some of the best of the Federal troops had been concentrated upon the single effort to turn Jackson's forces on the Rebel left, with whom, as we have stated, the tide of battle ebbed and flowed alternately. His men fought desperately—perhaps as they never fought before. Whole brigades were swept away before the fiery storm, and the ground was covered with the wounded and the dead. At one time, Ewell's old division, overpowered by superior numbers, fell back. Being supported by other troops, who rushed into the gap and retrieved the loss, Ewell's men returned to the fight, added their weight to that of their enthusiastic comrades, and in turn drove back the Federals. About the time when General Stark was killed, Lee ordered to the support of Jackson, McLaws's division, which had been held in reserve. It came most opportunely. Jackson's men had fought until not they alone, but their ammunition also, was well nigh exhausted, and discomfiture stared them in the face. Encouraged by the assistance of fresh troops, every man rallied and fought with redoubled vigor. They swept on like a wave—its billows rolling thick and fast upon the columns that had so stubbornly forced their way to the position on which the Rebels had originally commenced the battle—and regained the greater part of the ground which they had originally lost.

The fighting in this part of the field had been for many hours so excessive that the combatants were too exhausted to continue the strife. The contest here closed with scarcely any advantage being derived by either side. Some cornfields and woods, the occupation of which had been hotly contested during the day, were at its close held by the Federals, who took possession of the ghastly harvest which had been reaped, and which was strewn upon the ground.

The brunt of battle was now transferred to the opposite wings, commanded respectively by Burnside and D. H. Hill. As Jackson took no part therein, we will only briefly describe this section of the battle. To Burnside had been intrusted the difficult task of carrying the bridge near Rohrback's farm and assaulting the Rebel right. He received his instructions at ten o'clock in the morning, but up to three o'clock he had made little progress, beyond having successfully carried the bridge. At the last-named hour he advanced, and drove the Rebels before him nearly as far as Sharpsburgh. At this point the latter were reënforced by A. P. Hill, who opportunely arrived with the force that Jackson had left behind at Harper's Ferry, and Burnside was compelled to fall back. The fighting in this part of the field was almost entirely between artillery.

As the day was drawing to a close, McClellan was hastening from the centre to the left. He was met by a courier from Burnside, with the message : "I want troops and guns. If you do not send them I cannot hold my position for half an hour." Porter's corps was the only one in reserve left to the army, and it would have been dangerous to have sent it to Burnside's relief. McClellan glanced at the western sky, and then said slowly : "Tell General Burnside this is the battle of the war. He must hold his ground till dark at any cost. I will send him Miller's battery. I can do nothing more. I have no infantry." When the messenger was riding away, he called him back. " Tell him if he *cannot* hold his ground, then the bridge to the last man! always the bridge! If the bridge is lost, all is lost."

As the light faded the cannonade died away, and before it was quite dark the battle was over. After fourteen hours of hard fighting, all that the Federals had been enabled to accomplish was to turn the Rebel line on one flank, and secure a footing within it on the other. Both armies slept on their arms. Both commanders expected that the battle would be renewed on the following day, but neither was willing to commence the attack. So exhausted were their troops, that both felt glad to be able to escape a continuance of the contest. Upon the eighteenth General McClellan gave orders for a renewal of the attack at daylight on the following morning, but during that night the Confederate army was moved to the Virginia shore of the Potomac, and morning found a wide river separating the contending forces.

The Federal loss in the battle of South-Mountain was four hundred and forty-three killed, and one thousand eight hundred and six wounded; and in the battle of Antietam two thousand and ten killed, nine thousand four hundred and sixteen wounded, and one thousand and forty-three missing; making a total loss, in the two battles, of fourteen thousand seven hundred and ninety-four. We have no data from which to state the actual Confederate loss, but from the number of their dead who were left upon the field and were buried by the Federals, it was without doubt considerably greater than that of the National army.

Thirteen guns and thirty-nine colors more than fifteen thousand stand of small arms, and upward of six thousand prisoners, were the trophies obtained by the Federals.

The battle of Antietam was an unfinished one, consequently it was not a decisive one. It can hardly be claimed as a great victory if we are to judge of it by the results. It is true, however, that the Federals gained a little in the matter of space, and held at the close some important positions, which the Rebels had occupied at the beginning of the day. The losses which took place were of more serious import to the Rebels than they were to the Federals, as any reënforcements which the former could receive were too far away to be immediately available, whilst those of the latter were within reach. This doubtless led Lee to avoid risking another engagement, and to adopt the only course left open to him to ward it off—remove his army beyond the borders of Maryland.

To throw every obstacle in the way of the Federal army was naturally the desire of the Confederates. In this Jackson was remarkably prominent. Almost within gun-shot of McClellan's army, with a force not exceeding seven thousand, he destroyed thirty miles of the Baltimore and Ohio Railroad track, from seven miles west of Harper's Ferry to the North Mountain. He actually obliterated the road, so that when the road-masters with their gangs went to work to restore it, it was only by the charred and twisted *debris* that the track could be traced. Every tie was burned, every rail bent—nothing remained to be done but to cart off the bare ballast. The General took off his coat, and, with a cross-tie for a fulcrum and a rail for a lever, helped to demolish the "permanent way," and with his own hands he assisted in bending the heated rails around the trunks of trees. When all this rail-stripping and burning and twisting was done, Jackson walked over the whole thirty miles of his work to see that it was done thoroughly. He looked upon that road with the eye of a military genius, well aware of its great importance as a military thoroughfare. The prominent part it must play in the warlike machinery of the Government was plain to him; therefore he took the greater pains to destroy it totally.

A week after the battle of Antietam, General McClellan caused a reconnoissance to be made on the Virginia side of the Potomac, in the neighborhood of Shepherdstown, so that information might be obtained of the Rebel position and force in that vicinity. The troops, consisting of a brigade, with a portion of three regiments, and a battery, had their crossing at Blackford's Ford disputed by a few field-pieces. These were soon silenced, and the gunners took to flight, after which no enemy was visible. When the Federals were fairly landed, Jackson suddenly appeared in large force from ambush in the adjoining woods and opened upon them with shot and shell. The numbers were so unequal that although the Federals at first stood their ground, they were eventually compelled to retreat hastily, and recross the river under the Rebel fire. In this unfortunate affair the Federal killed, wounded, and missing numbered three hundred and twenty-six out of a force of about seventeen hundred.

The Confederates did not tarry many days upon the banks of the Potomac. After holding Harper's Ferry for less than a week they evacuated it, having first removed much of the property which they had captured, and destroyed some of the public buildings. They then retreated up the valley of the Shenandoah, from which they proceeded by the mountain passes into Eastern Virginia, where they once more took up their position on the banks of the Rappahannock.

# CHAPTER XI.

## THE BATTLE OF FREDERICKSBURGH.

Jackson's Antagonists—Burnside supersedes McClellan—The Army of the Potomac marches to the Rappahannock—The Battle-Ground—The Federals cross the River—Positions of the two Commanders—Advance of Franklin—Heroism of a Confederate Officer—Opening of the Battle—Sublimity of the Scene—Attack on the Fortifications—The Field of Death—The Combat described—Reserves brought into Action—The Losses—Councils of War—The River recrossed.

IT was Jackson's fortune, during his short but brilliant military career, to have crossed swords with some of the best and bravest of the Federal Generals. Thus far in our narrative we have found him opposed by Lander, on the Upper Potomac; by McDowell at Bull Run; by Shields, and Banks, and Fremont in the Virginian Valley; by Porter and Heintzelman, with McClellan as their chief, in the eventful conflicts near Richmond; by Pope, from the Rapidan to the lines of Washington; and by Hooker and Sumner, with McClellan again as chief, at the battle of Antietam. The remainder of his career we shall find passed upon a still different field, on which his might and military genius were resisted by still different Generals.

On the fifth of November the army of the Potomac was subject to a change of commanders. It was on that day

8*

ordered, by direction of the President, "that Major-General McClellan be relieved from the command of the army of the Potomac, and that Major-General Burnside take the command of that army."

This army had remained in the neighborhood of Harper's Ferry until near the end of October, when it commenced its march by the upper gaps of the Blue Ridge to Warrenton. After Burnside took command, it removed from the latter place to Falmouth, on the northern bank of the Rappahannock, by which river it is separated from the town of Fredericksburgh. On the twenty-first of November, General Sumner, who commanded the advance, demanded the surrender of the last-named town, but his request was not complied with.

It was General Burnside's intention to have crossed the Rappahannock at once, and taken possession of the heights above Fredericksburgh before General Lee was able either to concentrate his forces there or to fortify the position. The delay in the arrival of pontoon-bridges beyond the time anticipated compelled General Burnside to postpone active operations, and gave the Confederates sufficient time to gather together their army and erect fortifications.

After nearly a month of preparation, the Federal commander felt himself in a position to cross the river on the eleventh of December. At this date, General Lee, being deceived in the point where the river would be crossed, had rapidly despatched Jackson with a large portion of the army to a spot fifteen or twenty miles down the river, and D. H.

Hill with another portion of it in the opposite direction, in anticipation of the Federals crossing at one or other of those neighborhoods. Finding the Confederate forces thus divided, General Burnside hoped that by rapidly throwing over the whole of his command close to Fredericksburgh he would be enabled to fight the enemy in detail, and gain possession of the heights commanding the town. That this plan did not succeed is probably owing to the delay of a whole day in moving the army across the river, which delay was caused by the stubborn resistance of a brigade of Mississippi riflemen under General Barksdale, who thrice by their deadly fire compelled the Federals to abandon the attempt. This delay enabled Jackson and Hill to rapidly countermarch their forces and join the main army.

The battle of Fredericksburgh may be conveniently divided into two parts, in each of which the scene of action and the actors were distinct. It will render our narrative more intelligible to the reader if we lay before him separate descriptions of these two scenes of action, and of the combatants who met upon them.

The opposing armies that were to meet in deadly encounter were thus divided : General Burnside's army was divided into three grand divisions, under the respective commands of Generals Sumner, Franklin, and Hooker. General Lee's army was divided into two large *corps d'armée*, commanded respectively by Generals Longstreet and Jackson.

The theatre of operations extended from the town of

Fredericksburgh on the west, and along the south side of the Rappahannock for two miles to the east.

The stage on which the western battle was fought was immediately behind the town. Here the land forms a plateau, or smooth field, running back for about a third of a mile. It then rises for forty or fifty yards, forming a ridge of ground, which runs along to the east for about a quarter of a mile, where it abuts at Hazel Dell, a ravine formed by the Hazel River, which empties into the Rappahannock east of the town. At the foot of the ridge runs the telegraph-road, flanked by a stone wall. This eminence was studded with Rebel batteries. To the west, along up the river, the ridge prolongs itself to opposite Falmouth, and beyond; and here, too, batteries were planted on every advantageous position. Back of the first ridge is another plateau, and then a second terrace of wooded hills, where a second line of fortifications were placed. Between the rear of the town and the first ridge a canal runs right and left, and empties into the river some distance above Falmouth. The plain between the suburbs of the city and the first ridge of hills was the scene of encounter between General Sumner's forces and those of General Longstreet. General Hooker's division, which had been held in reserve on the northern side of the river, reënforced Sumner toward the close of the day.

The eastern battle-field was a short distance down the river. The ridge upon which the town is built slopes abruptly in this direction to a comparatively level or undulating country, which stretches for some miles down the Rap-

pahannock. This plain is bordered on the south by thickly
wooded heights, situated about two miles from the river.
Upon these heights Rebel batteries were placed. The
battle-ground, though very marshy in some places, presented a fine field for military evolutions. The turnpike
leading to Fredericksburgh runs about half a mile from and
nearly parallel to the river. Beyond is the railroad, and
still farther beyond the woody range of hills in which the
Rebels were strongly intrenched. On this battle-ground
General Franklin was met by General Jackson. The latter's forces were thus placed: A. P. Hill on the left, and
next to Longstreet's command; behind A. P. Hill, D. H.
Hill was held in reserve. Ewell's division, now commanded by General Early, held the woody heights, with Walker's artillery in his front, and Stuart's cavalry and horse-
artillery on his extreme right.

The Federal army had for some days been coiling itself
up into a small space, and on the morning of Thursday, the
eleventh of December, lay closely huddled together opposite to Fredericksburgh. Before daylight tents were struck
and knapsacks packed, and the troops prepared to cross the
river. The Rebels opened their fire upon the pontooners, and
stoutly resisted the laying of the bridges. The firing was
replied to by the Federals, who shelled the town for several
hours. The Seventh Michigan regiment, who volunteered
for the purpose, were sent across the river in boats to dislodge the Rebel sharp-shooters, who were picking off the
bridge-builders. After several ineffectual attempts, the

bridges were completed, and during Thursday night and throughout Friday the river was crossed by the Federal troops. The right grand division, under Sumner, crossed upon three pontoon-bridges, placed opposite the city, and the left grand division, under Franklin, upon two pontoon-bridges, placed about two miles down the stream. The centre grand division, under Hooker, comprising forty thousand men, was held in reserve upon the north bank of the river.

But little firing took place on Friday. Either General Lee wished to avoid damaging the town, which was at the time in possession of the Federals, or he was desirous of offering no further obstacle to the crossing, in the hopes that when he had got the Federal army between himself and the river, he would be enabled either to crush it or drive it into the stream. The Federals occupied the day in massing their troops, and in preparing for the coming struggle. Their siege-guns on the north side of the river at times fired upon the intrenchments of the Rebels, with the view of learning their position, but General Lee did not feel inclined to reply to the fiery interrogatories.

General Burnside's proposed plan of attack was that the battle should be opened by Franklin, who should advance and take possession of a road in the rear of the line of heights, which road formed a connecting link between Jackson's and Longstreet's commands. This position being gained, it was supposed that the Rebels would be so much confounded that Sumner could successfully storm and capture their intrenchments in the rear of Fredericksburgh. That this plan did not succeed, it is stated, is owing to Franklin having misunderstood his instructions, and having made the attack with an insufficient force.

Saturday the thirteenth dawned hazily, the fog being such as at that time of the year generally prefaces a genial Indian summer's day. The day was to become an eventful one in American history. The two great actors in the drama placed themselves in conspicuous positions to watch its progress. General Burnside took his stand at the Phillips House, situated on an eminence a little to the north of the town. General Lee took up his position upon a hill south-east of the heights which command Fredericksburgh, and which hill, from its having been his usual station, bore his name.

At half-past eight General Lee, accompanied by his full staff, rode slowly along the front of the Confederate lines, from left to right, and then took up his station for a time in the rear of Jackson's extreme right. As soon as Franklin's advance could be seen through the fog, General Stuart moved up a section of his horse-artillery in front of the position occupied by Lee, and opened with effect upon the Federal flank. Stuart ordered Major John Pelham, his chief of artillery, to advance one gun considerably nearer to Franklin, and to open upon him. Major Pelham obeyed, and opened the fire of a twelve-pounder Napoleon gun with great precision and deadly effect upon the Federal flank. The galling discharges of this gun quickly drew upon it the fire of three of Franklin's field-batteries, while from across the river two other heavy batteries joined in the strife, and made Major Pelham and his gun their target. For hours not less than thirty Federal cannon strove to silence Pelham's pop-gun, but strove in vain. Pelham's unyielding and undemonstrative courage, and his composure under the deadliest fire, had long made him conspicuous, but never were his daring qualities the subject of more glowing eulogy than upon this occasion. General Lee exclaimed: " It is inspiriting to see such glorious courage in one so young." Major Pelham was not more than twenty-two. General Jackson remarked: " With a Pelham upon either flank, I could vanquish the world."

At a subsequent period of the day, General Lee assumed his station on the hill which bears his name, and there, in company with General Longstreet, calmly watched the repulse of the Federal efforts against the heights near which he stood. Occasionally General Jackson rode up to the spot and mingled in conversation with the other two leading Generals. Once General Longstreet exclaimed to him, " Are you not scared by that file of Yankees you have before you down there?" to which Jackson replied: " Wait till they come a little nearer, and they shall either scare me or I'll scare them."

The battle opened when the sun had let in enough light through the mist to disclose the near proximity of the Federal lines and field-batteries. The first shot was fired shortly before ten o'clock from the batteries in the Federal centre,

and was directed against General Hood's division of Longstreet's corps, which division was drawn up immediately on
Jackson's left, and was next to the large division commanded by General A. P. Hill. The Pennsylvania reserves, commanded by General Meade, advanced boldly under a heavy
fire against the Confederates, who occupied one of the copse-
wood spurs, and were for a time permitted•to hold it; but
presently the Confederate batteries opened on them, and a
determined charge of infantry drove the Federals out of the
wood in confusion, from which nothing could subsequently
rally them. Simultaneously a heavy fire issued from the
batteries of A. P. Hill and Early's divisions, which was
vigorously replied to by the Federal field-batteries. The
only advantage momentarily gained by Franklin in this
quarter, was on the occasion of the collapse of a regiment
of North-Carolina conscripts, who broke and ran, but whose
place was rapidly taken by more intrepid successors. The
cannonading then became general along the entire line.

A spectator of this part of the battle thus graphically
describes the conflict: "Such a scene, at once terrific and
sublime, mortal eye never rested on before, unless the bombardment of Sebastopol, by the combined batteries of
France and England, revealed a more fearful manifestation
of the hate and fury of man. The thundering, bellowing
roar of hundreds of pieces of artillery, the bright jets of
issuing flame, the screaming, hissing, whistling, shrieking
projectiles, the wreaths of smoke, as shell after shell burst
into the still air, the savage crash of round-shot among the

trees of the shattered forest, formed a scene likely to sink forever into the memory of all who witnessed it, but utterly defying verbal delineation. A direct and enfilading fire swept each battery upon either side, as it was unmasked; volley replied to volley, crash succeeded crash, until the eye lost all power of distinguishing the lines of combatants, and the plain seemed a lake of fire, a seething lake of molten lava, coursed over by incarnate fiends, drunk with fury and revenge."

Twice the Federals, gallantly led and handled by their officers, dashed against the forces of Generals A. P. Hill and Early, and twice they recoiled, broken and discomfited, and incapable of being again rallied to the fray. The Confederates drove them with horrid carnage across the plain, and only desisted from their work when they came under the fire of the Federal batteries across the river. Upon the extreme Confederate right, General Stuart's horse-artillery drove hotly upon the fugitives, and kept up the pursuit until after dark.

Upon the Confederate right, where the antagonists fought upon more equal terms than they did upon their left, the loss sustained by the Rebels was the greatest; but still it was not so great as that of their Federal assailants.

Meanwhile, the battle which had raged so furiously between the forces of Franklin and Jackson, was little more than child's play as compared with the onslaught made by Sumner and Hooker against Longstreet in the rear of Fredericksburgh.

During the first two hours of the conflict between Jackson and Franklin, Sumner's skirmishers had been briskly engaged. The force in Fredericksburgh had driven the Rebels out of the suburbs of the town, and rested their columns on the canal. The time had now come, in accordance with the Federal plan, to attempt an advance on the Rebel position. It was mid-day. The orders were to move rapidly, charge up the hill, and take the batteries at the point of the bayonet. Orders easy to give, but ah ! how hard of execution !

Here is a picture of the position which had to be stormed. A bare plateau of a third of a mile in width is required to be crossed by the storming party. In doing this they would be exposed to the fire of the enemy's sharp-shooters, posted behind a stone wall running along the base of the ridge ; to the fire of a double row of rifle-pits on the rise of the crest ; to the fire of the heavy batteries placed behind earthworks on the top of the hill ; to the fire of a powerful infantry force lying concealed behind these batteries ; to a plunging fire from the batteries on the lower range ; and to a double enfilading fire from

"Cannon to the right of them, cannon to the left of them."

The distance to be traversed was short, but how many obstacles there were in the way of its being passed scathless !

To French's division of Couch's corps was assigned the duty of making the first attempt to cross this fiery plain. This division was composed of the brigades of Kimball,

Morris, and Weber. It was supported by Hancock's division, consisting of the brigades of Caldwell, Zook, and Meagher. The men were formed under cover of a small knoll in the rear of the town, and skirmishers were deployed to the left toward Hazel Dell. At the same time, General Sturgis supported and moved up and rested on a point on the railroad.

The scene which was witnessed when French's troops rushed upon this plateau was truly fearful. "The moment they exposed themselves upon the railroad," writes one who viewed the same, "forth burst the deadly hail. From the rifle-pits came the murderously-aimed missiles; from the batteries, tier above tier, on the terraces, shot-planes of fire; from the enfilading cannon, distributed on the arc of a circle two miles in extent, came cross-showers of shot and shell.

"Imagine, if you can, for my resources are unequal to the task of telling you, the situation of that gallant but doomed division.

"Across the plain for a while they swept under this fatal fire. They were literally mowed down. The bursting shells make great gaps in their ranks; but these are presently filled by the 'closing up' of the line. For fifteen immortal minutes at least, they remain under this fiery surge. Onward they press, though their ranks grow fearfully thin. They have passed over a greater part of the interval, and have almost reached the base of the hill, when brigade after brigade of Rebels rise up on the crest and pour in fresh volleys of musketry at short-range. To those who, through the glass looked on, it was a perilous sight indeed.  Flesh and blood could not endure it.  They fell back shattered and broken, amid shouts and yells from the enemy.

"General French's division went into the fight six thousand strong; late at night he told me he could count but fifteen hundred!"

Again and again the Rebel battlements were attempted to be stormed, but each time with the same terrible result.  "Where is Franklin?" began to be the eager inquiry.  "Every thing depends on Franklin coming up on the flank."  Sumner sent a message begging Burnside that Franklin be directed to advance.  But Franklin could not advance.  He had enough to do at the time to hold his own, for Jackson had thrown in reënforcements, and was pushing hard to turn his left.

At four o'clock the reserves had not been sent into action.  Hooker's central grand division, comprising forty thousand men, were still on the north bank of the river.  At Sumner's request, General Burnside directed them to cross, which they immediately did, notwithstanding the Rebel fire directed upon the pontoons.  Half an hour afterwards, and prodigious volleys of musketry announced that Hooker with the reserves was engaged, but the last assaulting column had hardly got into action before the sun went down, and night closed around the clamorous wrath of the combatants.

The last assaulting column consisted of the divisions of Humphrey, Monk, Howard, Getty, and Sykes.  The last assault is thus described by the writer from whom we last quoted : "Creeping up on the flank by the left, Getty's troops succeeded in gaining the stone wall which we had been unable all day to wrench from the Rebels. The other forces rushed for the crest. Our field-batteries, which, owing to the restricted space, had been of but little use all day, were brought vigorously into play. It was the fierce, passionate climax of the battle. From both sides two miles of batteries belched forth their fiery missiles athwart the dark background of the night. Volleys of musketry were poured forth such as we have no parallel of in all our experiences of the war, and which seemed as though all the demons of earth and air were contending together. Rushing up the crest, our troops had got within a stone's throw of the batteries, when the hill-top swarmed forth in new reënforcements of Rebel infantry, who, rushing upon our men, drove them back. The turn of a die decides such situations. The day was lost! Our men retired. Immediately cannon and musketry ceased their roar, and in a moment the silence of death succeeded the stormy fury of ten hours' battle."

The morning had opened with a general want of confidence, and gloomy forebodings that the plan of battle was fraught with danger. It was difficult to comprehend that the Confederate fortifications could be successfully assailed from the front, and there were grave doubts as to whether the operations on the right and on the left could be made to harmonize. That these surmisings and these forebodings were not fallacious was evidenced by the result of the day's engagement. That the Federals suffered a severe defeat there need be no denial, and this too after they had brought the entire of their vast force into action, whilst their antagonists, from the impregnable position which they held, were enabled to repel their assault with half the number.

The Federal loss in the day's battles amounted to one thousand one hundred and fifty-two killed, between six and seven thousand wounded, and about seven hundred prisoners, which latter were paroled and exchanged for about the same number taken from the Confederates. The Confederate killed and wounded amounted to about eighteen hundred.

After the close of the engagement, councils of war were held at the headquarters of each army. At that called by General Burnside, and which was attended by Sumner, Hooker, and Franklin, the Commanding General proposed to renew the attack on the following morning, but he was induced to abandon his intentions at the earnest solicitations of his brother Generals. It is reported that during General Lee's council General Jackson slept throughout the proceedings, and that upon his being awakened and asked for his opinion, he curtly exclaimed : " Drive 'em in the river ! drive 'em in the river !"

On the two days succeeding the battle (Sunday and Monday) the time was principally occupied in burying the dead and caring for the wounded. There was little to disturb the quiet of these bright and breezy days, beyond the sounds of musketry from some skirmishing parties, and a little artillery firing.

It now became palpable to the Federal Generals, in consequence of the little opposition which Lee had offered to the crossing of the river, that he had been desirous of getting them between his intrenchments and the Rappahannock, so that he could eventually crush them. It was now advisable to get out of the trap into which they had fallen; consequently, at a council of war held on Monday, it was unanimously agreed upon that the river be recrossed that night. This decision was not made known to the troops until after they had arranged their bivouacs in the evening. It was necessary that the withdrawal should be accomplished silently and rapidly, and that every precaution should be taken to avoid observation, and thus escape drawing the Confederate fire. Intense darkness and a heavy storm favored the Federal retreat. Earth was strewn on the pontoon-bridges, to deaden the sound of the artillery as it passed over; but this expedient was barely necessary, as a gale of wind, blowing all night from the direction of the Rebel camp toward the Federal lines, rendered it impossible for any sound to reach the former from the river.

When some time after midnight, the stars had made their appearance in the sky, and the moon had risen to shed her pale light on the earth, the army of the Potomac had crossed the river and was rescued from the annihilation which the Rebel Generals had prepared and predicted for it. General Lee was compelled to admit that the masterly retreat of his army across the Potomac, after the battle of Antietam, had been surpassed by this successful passage of the Federal force across the Rappahannock.

# CHAPTER XII.

## THE BATTLE OF CHANCELLORSVILLE.

In every army promotion is sure to follow upon every successful display of military ability, unless the soldier who proves his claim to an increase of honor has already arrived at the highest rank in the service. In the Confederate army there were two degrees of rank superior to that which Jackson held at the battle of Fredericksburgh—Lieutenant-General and General. That battle gained him the first, death alone prevented him from obtaining the second. It was, therefore, under the dignified title of a Lieutenant-General that Jackson was known in the few remaining months of his short military career. It took but a year and a half for the man who, at the beginning of the rebellion was the Colonel of a Virginia regiment, to rise to the second rank in the army in which he served. But if promotion had been made

13*

to keep pace with his increase of renown, we have no hesitation in stating that the highest rank was that to which he was justly entitled. We fancy that the reason why he did not obtain the highest military title is attributable to the misfortune of birth. Had it been Jackson's lot to have been a scion of one of the proud Virginian families, instead of a humble son of the Old Dominion, there can be little doubt but that the case would have been far different. At any rate, he had the proud satisfaction of knowing that what honors he did receive were fairly earned by him, and that the Government under which he served owed him more for his services than he owed it for its honors.

Immediately after the battle of Fredericksburgh, General Sigel hastened to reënforce Burnside with the corps under his command, but no farther active operations were attempted until the close of the month. General Burnside then prepared for another aggressive movement which embraced an attack in front of Fredericksburgh, and a formidable raid of cavalry and light artillery, which was to threaten the communications of the Confederates, and divert their attention from the main attack. The execution of the movement was fixed for the last day of the year. The column destined to make the raid was actually in motion, when President Lincoln sent a despatch forbidding the movement, having been induced to do so in consequence of the protest of some of General Burnside's subordinate officers.

By Wednesday the twenty-first of January, the Federal commander was again prepared to move on Fredericks-

burgh. Every thing having been arranged, and the Rebels
having been completely deceived by feints, as to the point
at which the river was to be crossed, the army was put in
motion on Tuesday, with the intention of commencing active
operations early on Wednesday morning. However, a heavy
rain-storm and a tempest of wind occurred during the night,
and so moistened the roads as to render it impossible to
move either pontoons or artillery with the celerity demanded. This, added to the evident intentional delay of some of
the superior officers in the marching of their troops, gave
time to enable the Confederates to discover the Federal
movement, and rally their forces to avert it. The moment
for the surprise having thus passed, the movement was abandoned.

General Burnside having thus found himself thwarted
in his operations by officers under his command, and feeling himself not properly supported by the Government,
tendered his resignation, which was accepted, and on the
twenty-sixth of January the command of the Army of the
Potomac was transferred to General Hooker.

The snows and storms of winter were a barrier to any
military operations during the next three months. The opposing armies took up their winter-quarters on opposite
banks of the Rappahannock, and within sound of each
other's bugles. At the close of April, when the snow had
disappeared from the ground, and the winds of spring had
somewhat hardened the roads, the bristling bayonet and the
booming cannon were called on for more active duty than

that which for the past few months they had been accustomed to perform.

General Hooker having massed what he termed "the finest army on the planet," commenced the offensive operations of the year by a flank movement upon Fredericksburgh, for which a portion of his army crossed the Rappahannock above that place, and gained a position in its rear distant ten miles west by south, whilst another portion crossed a short distance below the town, and menaced it from that quarter. But in this grand game of strategy he had to play with a formidable antagonist. If General Lee was at first nonplussed by Hooker's manœuvres, he was soon able to grasp the situation on the military chess-board, and make the move which was most likely to checkmate his opponent. He abandoned his position in Fredericksburgh and the line for twenty miles down the Rappahannock, which he had held for months, changed his front, and presented his face instead of his back to the Federal commander.

General Hooker had adjusted his plan of procedure by the middle of April, but the unsettled weather, which is not uncommon to that month, prevented its being put into operation until Sunday the twenty-sixth. He had, however, kept his own council, and even his corps commanders were unacquainted with the nature of the duties which they would be called on to perform. By Monday morning the entire army was in motion; the vast area which it covered for miles and miles in extent was an animated scene. Tents were struck, camps broken up, log huts abandoned, and their recent occupants moved away on a dozen different roads, carefully concealing themselves from the Confederate view by marching through woods and behind the knolls and ridges of the broken ground along the Rappahannock. Long trains of artillery, packed mules, and ambulances, intermingled with the moving throng, and added to the picturesqueness of the scene.

Shortly after Hooker took command, he abandoned the disposition of his army into grand divisions, and introduced the corps organization instead, and his army was now composed of seven *corps d'armée.*

By Tuesday morning some idea of his plan was discernible. Three of the seven *corps d'armée*—Reynolds's, Sickles's, and Sedgwick's—had left their camps the night before, and taken up their positions two miles below Fredericksburgh, at the point where Franklin crossed in December. The corps of Meade, Slocum, and Howard (formerly Sigel's) had already moved up the river, and on Tuesday were in the neighborhood of Banks's and United States Fords, respectively eight and eleven miles above Fredericksburgh. It seemed probable that operations would be inaugurated at the points above and below Fredericksburgh, though it was doubtful where the main attack would be made. By these movements Hooker had divided his army, and placed a space of a dozen miles between the two parts, which caused them to be out of supporting distance of each other. He doubtless intended to make a demonstration at one point, and the real attack at the other. He was ultimately compelled to enter the lists with his antagonist at both points.

Before dawn of Tuesday, and under cover of a very heavy fog, the pontoons were laid across the river at the point below Fredericksburgh, with but little opposition from the Rebel rifle-pits. An effort to lay pontoons at a later hour, and lower down the river, was not so successful, and it was not until forty guns had been brought to bear upon the Rebel sharp-shooters that the pontoons could be successfully placed. One division of each of the army corps, commanded by Sedgwick and Reynolds, were sent across the river. The remaining four divisions left the cover of the fringe of hills which had sheltered them from the view of the Rebels, and by marching and countermarching round the crests, magnified their number to their enemy. This ruse had the effect of causing the Confederates to move their columns from down the river to the vicinity of Fredericksburgh. These consisted of Jackson's entire corps, which had been posted there as an army of observation. Jackson was now upon the field where he had given battle to Franklin the previous December, but in this case history was not to repeat itself, and he was not here to fight a second battle on the same ground.

Let us now turn our attention to the three corps which had moved up the river. On the night of Tuesday, between ten P.M. and two A.M., Howard's entire corps crossed the Rappahannock on the pontoon bridge at Kelly's Ford, twenty-seven miles above Fredericksburgh. At daylight

Slocum's corps followed, and during the forenoon Meade's corps was thrown across. The movable column then struck direct for Germania Ford on the Rapidan River, distant twelve miles. General Meade, however, instead of taking this direction, on passing the river struck a road diverging eastward, and made Ely's Ford on the Rapidan, eight miles nearer than Germania Ford, to the *embouchure* of that stream into the Rappahannock. Both columns having crossed the respective fords, moved on Chancellorsville, at the junction of the Gordonsville turnpike with the plank-road leading to Orange Court-House. Communication was kept up between the two movable columns by a squadron of Pleasanton's cavalry, while another part of the same horsemen moved on the right flank of the outer column to protect it from Rebel cavalry attacks. This manœuvre having uncovered United States Ford, (which lies between Kelly's Ford and Fredericksburgh—twelve miles from the latter,) Couch's corps, which had for three days been lying at that point, was passed over the Rappahannock by a pontoon bridge on Thursday, without any opposition or indeed any demonstration more formidable than a brass band playing "Hail Columbia." This force also converged toward Chancellorsville, and on Thursday night four army corps — namely, Howard's, Stevens's, Meade's, and Couch's—were massed at that point. The same night General Hooker with his staff reached Chancellorsville, and established his headquarters in the only house there.

The military movement had thus far been executed with

celerity and success, and it was certainly a signal achievement to have marched a column of seventy-five thousand men, each laden with sixty pounds of baggage, together with artillery and trains, thirty-six miles in two days; and to have bridged and crossed two streams, along a line which a vigilant enemy undertook to observe and defend, with a loss of perhaps half a dozen men, one wagon, and two mules.

That General Hooker was himself satisfied with his past proceedings is evidenced in an order which he issued upon reaching Chancellorsville. · In it he stated: "It is with heartfelt satisfaction that the General Commanding announces to the army that the operations of the last three days have determined that our enemy must ingloriously fly, or come out from behind their defences and give us battle on our own ground, where certain destruction awaits him."

On Friday morning General Hooker began the strategetic disposition of his force. It was formed in a line of battle of a triangular or redan shape, resting with its wings respectively on the Rappahannock, between Banks and United States Fords, and Hart's Creek, and having its apex at Chancellorsville.

The day was occupied with operations along the skirmish line and reconnoissances for the purpose of feeling the enemy.

The situation of Chancellorsville is in the middle of a clearing in the woods, which takes the form of an irregular ellipse, about a mile in length and half a mile in width.

The solitary house that makes up Chancellorsville stands almost in the middle of this opening. The ground in the region between here and Fredericksburgh is broken and wooded, there being occasional clearings in the forests. It rises as it nears Fredericksburgh, when it develops into bold heights. Its strategetic importance is derived from the fact that it covers the Gordonsville turnpike and the Orange Court-House plank-road, and threatens the line of Gordonsville.

This wild, dreary region is called the Wilderness, which name the Confederates have given to the battle which here took place.

Working parties of the Federals were employed during the whole of Friday night in throwing up breastworks, and the woods resounded with the strokes of a thousand axe-men felling trees for the purpose of constructing abattis. Similar working parties of the Rebels were engaged in like manner not half a mile distant. On Saturday morning both armies were well intrenched, and it became the question which of the two should come out and give battle.

Having followed General Hooker to the place where he was compelled to encounter the Confederates, we will now enter the camp of General Lee, and narrate his march to the scene of strife.

On Wednesday, the twenty-ninth of April, the Confederates discovered that General Hooker had broken up his camp at Falmouth, and that his troops had crossed the

13*

Rappahannock at the places we have already named. The discovery was not a satisfactory one, as General Lee was at the time not only deprived of his "old war horse," General Longstreet, but his force was less in numbers than it had been for some time. But the Rebels were relieved when they witnessed the unruffled calmness of their Commanding General, who, without bustle or agitation, made the necessary disposition of his forces for the purpose of warding off the blow with which he was threatened. General Early was left with his division to guard Fredericksburgh and its vicinity, whilst Lee and Jackson slowly marched westward along the turnpike and plank-roads in the direction of Chancellorsville.

From the evidence which General Hooker had given at the court of inquiry, relative to the defeat at Fredericksburgh the previous December, General Lee was in a measure somewhat enabled to define the Federal plan. He consequently held all his troops, except Early's division, closely in hand, and on Thursday threw up earthworks midway between Fredericksburgh and Chancellorsville, and there arrested the advance of Hooker's force.

On Thursday, however, General Stuart had somewhat delayed the advance of the Federals near Kelly's Ford by cutting the head of one of their columns. The Confederate General Anderson, who was stationed with his division at United States Ford, was on the same day compelled to fall back, recoiling before the immense Federal host which was approaching.

Hooker did not press Lee hotly, but in his turn fell slowly back toward Chancellorsville, followed still more slowly by the Confederates. On Thursday evening, Stuart attacked a small force of the Federals on the Spotsylvania road, and caused them to retire with some loss.

On Friday, the first of May, General Lee continued to advance, and General Hooker to fall back. But as the opposing forces neared Chancellorsville, the former penetrated the latter's purpose in retreating, when he discovered that about five hundred yards in front of that place, in the midst of a dense thicket of scrub-oak or black-jack, the Federal pioneers had thrown up very strong intrenchments at right angles to the turnpike and plank-roads, with an abattis of felled trees bristling outward in front, and seemingly defying the passage of any living and walking animal. Running southward for about a mile from the plank-road, the Federal works turned short to the west, until they again met the plank-road between Chancellorsville and Orange Court-House, toward the latter of which points the plank-road deflects in a south-westerly direction after leaving Chancellorsville. Within these works the Federals stood thickly and savagely at bay, their powerful artillery massed on some high ground a little in the rear. Their position was fearfully formidable—repulse, if the works were attacked solely from the front, seemed inevitable—the loss of life to the assailants anyhow must have been ghastly. Under these circumstances, General Lee resolved to outflank the flanker,

In the early part of Saturday several small engagements

took place at different parts of the lines, and toward the close of the day commenced the battle of Chancellorsville, which did not terminate until mid-day on Sunday. It was on Saturday evening that the subject of our memoir received those wounds which resulted in his death, and deprived the Confederate army of its most brilliant commander.

The movements of the Rebels seemed to indicate to the Federals that they were retreating, and as the main line of the retreat was occupied by the latter's forces, an attack to recover that line was confidently expected. The surprise of the Federals was consequently very great when, on Saturday afternoon, they found Jackson upon their extreme right and rear, between Chancellorsville and Germania Mills.

The particulars of this battle have been so graphically narrated by the Special Correspondent of *The* (London) *Times* in the Confederate States, who was present at the battle, that we have no hesitation in transferring it to these pages. He says:

"If ever man was adapted for the execution of a plan daring and hazardous in the extreme, but depending for its safety upon the celerity and audacity of its execution, assuredly that man was 'Stonewall' Jackson. With the first break of dawn he plunged with his three famous divisions— the first commanded by A. P. Hill; the second, in the absence of Trimble, by Coulson; the third, lately under D. H. Hill, by Rhodes—into the country-road which leads to the Furnace.* At the Furnace he ascended a hill, and was viewed

---

* A road which diverges from the plank-road two miles east of Chancel-

by the enemy from an adjoining hill, called Fairview, and heavily though harmlessly shelled. With his usual temerity he sent back word to General Lee that the Furnace hill must be held by one regiment until his artillery and wagons had got by. A South-Carolina regiment was accordingly sent there, but was, I believe, shortly carried forward in company with the cavalry, and in its place three or four companies of a Georgia regiment were left to guard the critical spot. The enemy discovering the weakness of the guard, attacked and took the Georgians prisoners. The last of Jackson's batteries was passing as the Georgians were captured, whereupon Captain Brown unlimbered his guns, opened on the Federals, and drove them back. He then passed on after Jackson, whose wagons had to fall back and pursue their General by a more circuitous route. Marvellous to say, it never seems to have suggested itself to General Hooker, although this large body of Confederates passed under his nose, that his rear was in danger, or that General Lee, greatly weakened, was lying within a few hundred yards of the mighty Federal host of eighty thousand men.

"At four in the afternoon General Lee, knowing that Jackson could not be far from his destination, opened fire steadily along his whole line, feeling the gigantic masses of his intrenched foe. For two hours and a half a heavy fire was interchanged between the hostile batteries, each party holding its own line. Suddenly, about half-past six in the

lorsville, and enters it again five miles to the west of that place. In this road is situated a foundry called the Catherine Furnace.

evening, the rattle of musketry was heard in the distance, followed by the loud boom of artillery, and instantly General Lee passed word along his lines : ' Jackson at work; press them heavily everywhere.' Swift and sudden as the falcon swooping on her prey, Jackson had burst on his enemy's rear, and crushed him before resistance could be attempted. Passing right over the plank-road, and extending almost up to the Ely's Ford road, getting behind Chancellorsville, the three noble divisions raced gallantly forward, drunk with the animal joy and inebriation of battle. Not a trench had been dug, not a tree felled, not a stick raised to resist them. The unconscious Federals, engaged in cooking their supper— one regiment on dress-parade—heard in the sudden volley of Jackson's long line the knell of their doom. An intelligent Virginia farmer, Mr. Green, taken prisoner by the Federals, heard one of their Generals say to his men about six o'clock : ' Jackson and his rebels don't dare face us to-night. Get your supper ready, boys, and enjoy yourselves.' With faces turning eastward, secured, as they fancied, by the dense masses of their friends within the intrenchments in front, without a thought of their rear, the Federals rummaged their knapsacks for all the luxuries with which Boston, New-York, and Philadelphia pamper and recruit their Sybarite soldiers. Before that supper could be eaten, the unwashed, unkempt, starving ragamuffins of the South had burst on them from the west, and scattered them, nerveless, panic-stricken, helpless, like chaff before the blast. Major Reyton, of General Lee's staff, found a coffee-pot, with cups round it, standing in the wood. He poured the liquid out, but it was so hot he could not drink it. What might have been the result but for one casualty, which alone almost counterveiled the victories of a week, who shall say? Formation or order the Federals had none; reserves, tactics, organization, disposition, plan, all went down before the whirlwind suddenness of the surprise. The loss of the Confederates was ludicrously small; their advance like that of a white squall in the bay of Naples.

"Night had fallen. About eight o'clock General Jackson rode forward with two or three of his staff along the plankroad, and advanced one hundred and fifty yards in front of his foremost skirmishers, peering with those keen eyes which you might fancy could be seen through the densest gloom forward into the night. He turned to ride back—a heavy fire from one of his own regiments, hailing from South-Carolina, but whose number I will in mercy withhold, saluted him. One bullet struck his left arm four inches below the shoulder, shattering the bone down to the elbow. The wound was intensely painful; he half fell, half was lifted from his horse. An aid galloped back to A. P. Hill to report that Stonewall Jackson was wounded and lying in the road. General Hill galloped hastily up, flung himself from the saddle, began, choked with emotion, to cut the cloth of Jackson's sleeve, when suddenly four of the Federal videttes appeared on horseback, and were fired on by the staff-officers. The videttes fell back upon a strong and swiftly advancing line of Federal skirmishers. General Hill and all the officers and couriers of both staffs had no alternative but to mount and ride for their lives, leaving Jackson where he lay. Right over the ground where was stretched the wounded lion the Federals advanced. Within their grasp lay the mightiest prize, the most precious jewel in the Confederate crown; but it was not destined that Stonewall Jackson should be struck by a Federal bullet, or yield himself prisoner to a Federal soldier. As General Hill and his companions galloped back they also became the target of the same luckless North-Carolinians. General Hill's boot was cut by a bullet, but his leg uninjured; Colonel Crutchfield, Chief of Artillery to Jackson, was seriously if not mortally wounded; Boswell, of Jackson's staff, killed; Howard, Engineer to A. P. Hill, knocked from his horse, but whether killed, or wounded, or a prisoner, is not known; two or three couriers killed. Without losing a moment, General Hill threw his own skirmishers forward, backed by heavy supports, and the ground on which lay General Jackson was again occupied by the Confederates. But in the mean time two more bullets, both from his own men, had struck him as he lay on the ground, one passing through the wrist of his shattered arm, the other entering the palm of his right hand and coming out through its back. He was at once carried to the rear and his arm instantly amputated under chloroform.

"Never was it more apparent than this evening what Jackson's presence and influence are to his men. With his wound ceased the fiery desperation of their onslaught; tidings of it flew like wildfire through the ranks; the routed

Federals found themselves no longer closely pressed, and took heart of grace as they poured grape and canister down the plank-road. Between nine and ten General A. P. Hill was struck by a bit of shell on the calf of his leg, which caused a painful contusion, and forced him reluctantly from the field. At ten P.M., General J. E. B. Stuart was by General Lee withdrawn from his cavalry command, and put temporarily at the head of General Jackson's corps, stripped as it was of the two leading Generals who have hitherto partaken its dangers and glories without being arrested by disease or stricken by bullet."

The same writer thus describes the appearance of the field upon which Jackson received his death-wound, as viewed by him after the termination of the battle:

"With astonishing accuracy Stuart's enfilading fire had torn through their ranks. In every variety of attitude of death, torn, rent, and shivered into scarcely distinguishable humanity, lay what so lately had breathed and moved. Still more terrible and strangely appalling was the road from Chancellorsville toward Orange Court-House, along which and on either side of which Jackson had descended to the harvest of death. Tumbrlls overthrown, caissons exploded, horses dead and dying, sometimes with broken legs, sometimes with ghastly wounds; human bodies in every guise of suffering and death, tortured and riven trees, and, most fearful of all, a crackling fire, running swiftly through the grass and black-jack brushwood, and suggesting dreadful thoughts of wounded and helpless men perishing by the most agonizing death known to humanity, froze the blood with horror, as the spectator in agony turned his eyes to heaven, to gain a moment's relief from the unutterable and woeful anguish of earth."

A quarter of an hour previous to the discharge of the fatal shots which deprived Jackson of his life, a Federal officer, who was wounded and taken prisoner, appeared before him. This officer was Captain Wilkins, of the staff of General A. S. Williams, who commanded a division of the National Army. The particulars of the interview between that officer and General Jackson are here given, as we find them narrated in a Northern journal:

" When captured, Captain Wilkins was placed in charge of a guard, who took him a short distance to the rear, where he met General Jackson and staff. Jackson was sitting on his horse at the head of the column, surrounded by his staff. He wore a new suit of gray uniform, and was a spare man with a weather-beaten face and a bright, grayish-blue eye. He had a peculiarly sad and gloomy expression of countenance, as though he already saw a premonition of his fate. It was but fifteen minutes later that he was mortally wounded. As they came into his presence the guard announced: 'A captured Yankee officer.' Captain Wilkins asked if it was Major-General Thomas J. Jackson. On being answered in the affirmative, he raised his hat. General Jackson said: 'A regular army officer, I suppose—your officers do not usually salute ours.' Captain Wilkins replied: 'No, I am not; I salute you out of respect to you as a gallant officer.'

He then asked his name and rank. On being told, he further inquired what corps and commanders were opposed in front. Captain Wilkins replied that, as an officer, he could not return a truthful answer to such questions. Jackson then turned to the guard and ordered them to search him. He then had in the breast-pocket of his coat Hooker's confidential orders to corps commanders, giving a plan in part of the campaign; the countersigns of the field for a week in advance, and the field returns, giving the effective strength of the Twelfth corps (Slocum's) on the preceding day. These were all exceedingly important papers.

"Fortunately, before the guard could carry the orders into execution, a terrific raking fire was opened on Jackson's column by twenty pieces of artillery, from an eminence on the plank-road. The first eight or ten shots flew over the heads of the column. The men and gunners dismounted, leaving horses and guns. Our artillery soon got the range with more precision, and the shell and round shot ricochetted and ploughed through this dense mass of the enemy with terrific effect. Shells were continually bursting, and the screams and groans of the wounded and dying could be heard on every side. As an instance of the terrible effect of this fire, one of the guard was struck by a solid shot just below the hips, sweeping off both his legs. A battery came dashing up, but when they got into the vortex of the fire the gunners fled, deserting their guns, and could not be made to man them. An officer, splendidly mounted and equipped, attempted, in a most gallant manner, to rally them. A ball struck him on the neck, completely severing his head from his body and leaving his spinal column standing. His body rolled to the ground, and the horse galloped to the rear. One of the shells struck a caisson full of artillery ammunition, which, exploding, ascended in a crater of various colored flame, and showered down on the heads of the men below a mass of fragments of shot and shell. The loss inflicted by this fire must have been terrible, placing considerable over one thousand men *hors du combat* and effectually breaking up the contemplated attack of the column.

" While Captain Wilkins was being taken to the rear he devoted his attention to disposing of the important papers which he had on his person. He dare not take them from his pocket to attempt to tear them up, but continuously placed his hand in his pocket and worked the papers into a ball, and as they were passing along, got them into his bosom, and finally into the arm-pit under his arm, where he carried them all that night. The next morning the guard halted to get their breakfasts, and a soldier was trying to kindle a fire to cook some coffee which they had taken from our men. The wood was damp and the fire refused to burn. The soldier swore at it until his patience gave out, when Captain Wilkins asked him if he would not like some kindlings, and handed him the important papers. The soldier took them, and, not dreaming of their importance, used them to kindle the fire."

Our narrative is drawing to a close. The military career

of Thomas Jonathan Jackson has terminated. But we have yet to be silent watchers by the bedside of the dying soldier, and to accompany his remains to the tomb. However, before we enter upon a description of the mournful scenes which are left to us to narrate, it is necessary that we should briefly sum up the remaining events which occurred between the opposing armies, before the series of conflicts which were initiated by the engagement of the first of May were brought to an end.

The portion of Hooker's army which was broken by Jackson's onslaught, and which so ingloriously fled from the battle-field, was Howard's corps, formerly commanded by General Sigel. These troops have been subject to much censure for their conduct on this occasion, but they claim that if they had not been deceived in the position of the enemy, and had not been deprived of their cavalry, by which they could have learned the true position of the Rebels in their front, the disaster would not have taken place.

Fighting took place during the greater part of the night that Jackson fell, and continued with increased fury during Sunday morning, when the Federals were driven within their breastworks. On that day General Sedgwick's troops captured the heights in the rear of Fredericksburgh, and emboldened by their success over Early's division, followed it on the road for a short distance toward Chancellorsville. On Monday, General Lee being satisfied that Hooker would not further give him battle, repaired to Fredericksburgh, and, in person, marshalled the brigades of the three divisions in that part of the field. That evening he drove Sedg-wick back with great slaughter, when the latter repaired to Banks's Ford and crossed the river. The day had been a quiet one at Chancellorsville, and on the following morning General Hooker, being satisfied that his attempt to capture the Confederate army was a failure, retired from his posi-tion, and sought refuge on the northern bank of the Rappa-hannock.

In connection with these military proceedings, a dashing cavalry raid was made by General Stoneman, who ap-proached within a few miles of Richmond, and severed Lee's communications by railway with that place.

The Federal losses in the engagements which took place in these early days of May were extremely heavy, and num-bered about twenty-five thousand in killed, wounded, and missing. The Confederates estimated their loss at one thousand killed, four thousand wounded, and one thousand prisoners. They claim to have captured from the Federals seven thousand six hundred and fifty prisoners. On the other hand, General Hooker stated in a general order, issued after the battles: "We have taken from the enemy five thousand prisoners and fifteen colors, captured and brought off seven pieces of artillery, and placed *hors du combat* eighteen thousand of his chosen troops."

But the Confederates suffered one loss which was to them irretrievable. We need not say that that was the loss of General Jackson. General Lee considered the deprivation of his services so great that, before he was aware that the accident would result in death, he exclaimed to a friend: "Had I been able to dictate events, most gladly would I have been disabled in my own person if he had been spared. Such an executive officer the sun never shone on. I have but to show him my design, and I know that if it can be done it will be done. No need for me to send and watch him. Straight as the needle to the pole he advances to the execution of my purpose. Pure, high-minded, unselfish, he has no earthly thought of himself or his own advancement. The sole aim and object of his life is the good of his country."

# CHAPTER XIII.

## LAST MOMENTS AND OBSEQUIES.

WHILE General Jackson was being carried on a litter to the rear of the battle-field at Chancellorsville, one of the bearers was shot down, and the wounded soldier fell from the shoulders of the men. This fall caused him to receive a severe contusion, which, added to the injury of his arm, created severe pain in his side. The General was left on the ground for five minutes, until the fire under which they were situated slackened. He was then placed in an ambulance and carried to the field-hospital at Wilderness Run. On being conveyed thither, frequent inquiries were made by the soldiers: "Who have you there?" He said to the doctor: "Do not tell the soldiers that I am wounded."

From the large amount of blood which he lost, he fancied that he was dying, and stated so to Dr. McGuire. It was feared that he would have bled to death, consequently a tourniquet was immediately applied to stop the further effusion of blood. The shock which he had received rendered him nearly pulseless for the space of two hours. After the reäction, a consultation was held between the surgeons present, and it was decided that amputation of the arm was necessary. Jackson was asked: "If we find amputation necessary, shall it be done at once?" He replied: "Yes, certainly, Dr. McGuire; do for me whatever you think is right." He bore the operation, which was performed while he was under the influence of chloroform, extremely well.

On Sunday morning, after a good sleep, the wounded soldier was cheerful, and in every way was doing well. He desired that his wife should be sent for, and asked minutely about the battle. He spoke cheerfully of its result, and said smilingly: "If I had not been wounded, or had had an hour more of daylight, I would have cut off the enemy from the road to the United States Ford, and we would have had them entirely surrounded, and they would have been obliged to surrender, or cut their way out. They had no other alternative. My troops sometimes may fail in driving the enemy from a position, but the enemy always fail to drive my men from a position."

His chaplain left him during the morning to go and perform service before the troops. The text was suggested by General Jackson, and was taken from Romans viii. 28: "We know that all things work together for good to them that love God." It was one of the General's favorite texts, and furnishes a key to the character of his religious belief.

Not for one moment did he question or murmur when struck down at the zenith of his fame. "I consider these

10

wounds a blessing. They were given me for some good and wise purpose. I would not part with them if I could." Such was substantially the language he used during the last few days of his life.

He complained on Sunday of the effects of the fall from the litter on the previous day, but no contusion or abrasion was apparent as the result thereof. However, he did not complain of his wounds, and never spoke of them unless when they were alluded to.

Jackson slept well on Sunday night, and on Monday was carried to Chancellor's house near Gurness's dépôt. He was cheerful during the day, conversed about the battle, and inquired after all his officers. During his removal, he complained greatly of the heat, and begged that a wet cloth be applied to his stomach, which was done and added greatly to his relief. He slept well that night, and relished his food the following morning.

On Monday he received the following note from General Lee, expressive of the regret the latter felt upon receiving intelligence of the accident that had befallen him:

CHANCELLORSVILLE, VA., May 4, 1863.

To Lieutenant-General T. J. JACKSON:

GENERAL: I have just received your note, informing me that you were wounded. I cannot express my regret at the occurrence. Could I have directed events, I should have chosen for the good of the country to have been disabled in your stead. I congratulate you upon the victory which is due to your skill and energy.

Most truly yours,    R. E. LEE, General.

On Tuesday, his wounds were proceeding very well. He asked: "Can you tell me, from the appearance of the wounds, how long I will be kept from the field?" He seemed much satisfied when he was told that they were doing remarkably well. During the day he did not complain of any pain in his side, and expressed a desire to see the members of his staff; but he was informed that such an interview would not be advisable.

As Jackson's wounds were progressing so favorably, it was intended to have removed him on Wednesday to Richmond, but the removal was prevented by a fall of rain. That night, while his attending surgeon, who had been deprived of rest for three nights, was asleep, the patient complained of nausea, and ordered his boy to place a wet towel over his stomach, which was done. The surgeon was awakened about daylight by the boy exclaiming: "The General is in great pain." The pain was in the right side, and resulted from incipient pneumonia and a slight degree of nervousness, which Jackson attributed to his fall from the litter.

On Thursday Mrs. Jackson arrived, greatly to the joy and satisfaction of the wounded hero, whom she faithfully nursed during the few remaining days of his life. By that evening all pain had ceased, but the patient suffered greatly from prostration. This prostration increased on the following day, but no pain was experienced. On Sunday morning it was apparent that Jackson was rapidly sinking, when it became necessary to intimate the same to his wife.

Mrs. Jackson was then allowed full and free converse with her husband. She told him that he was going to die, upon which he replied: "Very good, very good. It is all right."

The closing scene of Jackson's life bore a striking resemblance to that of the first Napoleon. While in the case of the great European Captain "the ruling passion was strong in death," it was none the less so in that of the Southern soldier. The battle-field, with all "the pomp and circumstances of war," was all before him, while what remained of life was ebbing fast. His mind wandered back, in the delirium of approaching dissolution, to the scenes of the battle. He gave the word of command, uttered words of encouragement to regiments staggering under fire, ordered his commissary to hasten on with needful food to exhausted troops. Almost the last sentence was the order he had so often given in life: "A. P. Hill, prepare for action."

Sunday, the tenth day of May, 1863, will ever be a day of mournful memory to the people of the sunny South. On that day set the most resplendent star in their galaxy of Generals. He, who had forsaken the quietude of the Professor's life to place himself at the head of charging columns, on that day breathed his last. He, who, amid the blaze of cannon, the rattle of musketry, and the clash of steel, had won honor and renown, died a soldier's death, and died as he had lived—strong in his religious faith. His years numbered only thirty-nine, but he had gained during the two closing years of his life more of military glory than is won by many whose lives are permitted to be extended to three-score years and ten.

General Jackson's death was officially announced to the army in which he served by the following order, which was issued by the Commanding General:

GENERAL ORDERS—NO. 61.

HEADQUARTERS, NORTHERN VIRGINIA, May 11, 1863.

With deep grief the Commanding General announces to the army the death of Lieutenant-General T. J. Jackson, who expired on the tenth instant, at a quarter-past three P.M. The daring, skill, and energy of this great and good soldier, by an all-wise Providence, are now lost to us. But while we mourn his death, we feel that his spirit still lives, and will inspire the whole army with his indomitable courage and unshaken confidence in God as our hope and strength. Let his name be a watchword to his corps, who have followed him to victory on so many fields. Let the officers and soldiers imitate his invincible determination to do every thing in the defence of our beloved country.

R. E. LEE, General.

When Jackson felt that death was approaching, and that his corps would soon be deprived of its commander, he frequently expressed to his aids his desire that General Ewell, in whom he had great confidence, might be appointed his successor. In accordance with this desire, General Ewell received the appointment.

In no city of the South was General Jackson more greatly respected than in the Confederate capital. So anxious were the people of Richmond to be informed of the daily condition of the illustrious chieftain, that on the Sunday upon which he died, his critical position was announced from the pulpits of many churches. This announcement prepared the people for the mournful intelligence which was so soon to follow; but it was for a time hard for them to believe in the correctness of such unwelcome news. It was to this city that Jackson's remains were removed after he had breathed his last.

Richmond clothed herself in mourning, and cast off the cares of business, so that she might fittingly receive the body of the departed hero. On Monday afternoon, a large concourse of ladies and gentlemen attended at the railway station to receive the corpse. It arrived about four o'clock, in charge of the following officers:

Of Lieutenant-General Jackson's staff:

Major S. Pendleton, Adjutant-General in charge; Dr. Hunter McGuire, Medical Director; Major W. J. Hawks, Lieutenants Morrison and Smith, Aids.

On the part of the army:

Major D. B. Bridgford, Captain H. K. Douglas.

On the part of the Commonwealth of Virginia:

Dr. John Mayo, Aid to the Governor, Colonel John C. Shields.

The coffin was covered with wreaths, which had been placed upon it by the ladies of Ashland as the remains passed that place. With as little delay as possible, the body was removed under military escort to the Governor's mansion, to which place it was followed by perhaps the largest assemblage of persons ever collected in Richmond.

On Tuesday, the last offices of honor to the departed hero were performed by the citizens of Richmond with fitting magnificence. We give the particulars of the proceedings, as we find them narrated in the Richmond *Enquirer* of the following day:

"In no public ceremony, not even the grand display which attended the inauguration of the monument to Washington some years ago, has Richmond been rendered more memorable than upon this occasion, when every branch of the Confederate and State Governments, with an army of bronzed and hardy heroes, and the whole city pouring forth its living tribute, aged and young of both sexes, joined in the pageant, and gave it all the imposing grandeur which sympathy, sorrow, love and admiration united, could bestow.

"In accordance with arrangements made upon Monday, the procession was formed upon Capitol Square at ten o'clock, stretching along Monument Avenue from the Governor's mansion, out upon Grace street, and consisted of the following civil and military bodies :

Public guard, with armory band, followed by the Nineteenth and Fifty-sixth Virginia Infantry, Major Wren's battalion of cavalry, and the Richmond Lafayette artillery, all preceded by a full band.

Hearse drawn by four white horses, appropriately caparisoned, the hearse draped and plumed, and the coffin wrapped and decorated with flowers.

Pall-bearers, consisting of the staff of the lamented hero,
and several other officers of high rank, wearing
the insignia of mourning.
Carriages, containing—first, His Excellency the President,
and the family of the deceased, followed by personal
friends and distinguished admirers; various chiefs
of Departments, State and Confederate; civil,
military, and judicial; the Mayor of the
city and members of the Council.

"On either side, and in the rear, an immense throng of ladies and gentlemen, children, servants and soldiers, mingled ready to move along with the procession. The banners were draped with crape, and the swords of the military officials were draped at the hilt. The artillery bore the sad insignia; the arms of the infantry were reversed; the drums were muffled, and at the given hour a gun stationed beneath the monument boomed forth the signal for motion.

"General George W. Randolph, Chief Marshal of the ceremony, proceeded to the front, and the cavalcade moved slowly out upon Governor street, through the Mansion Gate. The bells of the city commenced tolling, and soon a melancholy dirge swelled forth in moving tones from the leading corps of musicians. The procession passed down Governor to Main street, turning up the latter, and proceeding as far as Second street. The streets were crowded with people; stores were closed, as the pageant moved along, and from many windows floated flags draped in mourning. The flags upon the public buildings remained as on Monday, at half-mast. The scene on Main street was beyond adequate description, so impressive, so beautiful, so full of stirring associations, blending with the martial dirges of the bands, the gleam of musket, rifle, and sabre drawn, the sheen of black cannon, thousands of throbbing hearts, and the soul of sorrow that mantled over all. From Second street, through which the procession partly passed, it wheeled into Grace street, down which it returned to Capitol Square, entering by Monument Gate. At different stages of the obsequies the cannon, which remained stationed at the foot of the monument, pealed out in tones of thunder, which heightened the effect of the tolling bells, the solemn music, and the grand display.

"The hearse being drawn up in front of the Capitol, the coffin was removed to the hall of the House of Representatives, where it was laid in state in front of the Speaker's seat. Thousands crowded into the building, many bearing splendid bouquets with which to adorn the coffin, and at night hundreds were turned away, after hours of fruitless efforts, without seeing the face of the beloved departed warrior. All the courts in Richmond passed resolutions of respect to the memory of Jackson, and adjourned to attend the ceremonies."

Jackson had never seen his home since the war broke out; nor would he, he declared, until it was over, "unless the war itself should take him thither." The war *did* take him thither, but alas! it was not for him to *see* the place he loved so well. Richmond would fain have found a fitting

10*

resting-place for the remains of one she so much honored, but all that she was enabled to do was merely to pay them a passing tribute as they were being conveyed to their final home. Says the Richmond *Examiner:*

"All the poor honors that Virginia, sorely troubled and pressed hard, could afford her most glorious and beloved son, having been offered to his mortal part in this capital, the funeral *cortége* of the famous Jackson left it yesterday (Wednesday) morning, on the long road to 'Lexington, in the Valley of Virginia.' It was the last wish of the dead man to be buried there, amid the scenes familiar to his eyes through the years of his manhood, obscure and unrecorded, but perhaps filled with recollections to him not less affecting than those connected with the brief but crowded period passed upon a grander stage. This desire, expressed at such a time, demanded and has received unhesitating compliance. Yet many regret that his remains will not rest in another spot. Near this city is a hill crowned by secular oaks, washed by the waters of the river identified with what is great in the State's history from the days of Elizabeth to the present hour, which has been well selected as the place of national honor for the illustrious dead of Virginia. There sleep Monroe and Tyler. We have neither a Westminster nor a Pantheon, but all would wish to see the best that we could give conferred on Jackson. Hereafter, Virginia will build for him a stately tomb, and strike a medal to secure the memory of his name beyond the reach of accident, if accident were possible. But it is not possible; nor is a monument necessary to cause the story of this man's life to last when bronze shall have corroded and marble crumbled."

Jackson's remains reached Lexington on Thursday afternoon, having been escorted thither by a portion of his staff, the Governor of the State, and a committee from Lynchburgh. "They were received," says the Lynchburgh *Virginian*, "at the boat-landing by the corps of cadets, under General F. H. Smith, the professors of the Institute, and a large number of citizens, and were escorted in solemn procession to the Institute barracks, where they were deposited in the old lecture-room of the illustrious deceased. The room was just as he left it two years before, save that it was heavily draped in mourning—not having been occupied during his absence. The hall which so often echoed the voice of the modest and unknown professor, received back the laurel-crowned hero with the applause of the world and the benedictions of a nation resting upon him. It was a touching scene, and brought tears to many eyes, when the body was deposited just in front of the favorite chair from which his lectures were delivered. Professors, students, visitors, all were deeply moved by the sad and solemn occasion, and gazed in mute sorrow on the affecting spectacle of the dead hero lying in his familiar lecture-room. Guns were fired every half-hour during the day in honor of the departed chieftain, and an air of gloom was visible on every face."

The funeral took place on the next day, Friday, the fifteenth of May. The coffin was enveloped in the Confederate flag, and covered with flowers. It was borne on a caisson of the cadet battery, draped in mourning. The procession consisted of such officers and soldiers of the old Stonewall brigade as happened at the time to be in the county. It awakened thrilling associations to see the shattered fragments of this famous brigade assembled under the flag which for some time was the regimental standard of Jackson's old Fourth regiment, and which that regiment carried in triumph over the bloody field of Manassas on the ever memorable twenty-first day of July.

An interesting part of the ceremonies of the day were the religious services. These took place in the church in which the great chieftain had delighted to worship God for ten years before the beginning of his late brilliant career. They were conducted by the Rev. Dr. White, a pastor whom he tenderly loved, and whose religious counsels he modestly sought, even in the midst of the most absorbing scenes through which, during the last two years, he had passed.

The body was deposited in the cemetery connected with the church, where his first wife and child are buried.

There, within the borders of that quiet town in which had been spent the happiest and most peaceful moments of his life; there, under the shadow of that institution in which he had worked so assiduously, lie the remains of one that Lexington may well be proud to own. There, under the green Virginian sward, lies all that remains of one of Virginia's noblest sons.

# ADDENDA.

———•••———

SEVERAL incidents in Jackson's·life, and some sketches of his personal appearance and character, which, if inserted in the body of our work, would have interfered with the line of narrative, are here given in the form of a supplementary chapter.

An Englishman who had brought a box from Nassau to General Jackson, received an invitation to visit him in his camp. He did so in March last, and on his way thither experienced a drenching rain. He gives the following particulars of his visit:

"Wet to the skin, I stumbled through mud, I waded through creeks, I passed through pine-woods, and at last I got into camp about two o'clock. I then made my way to a small house occupied by the General as his headquarters. I wrote down my name and gave it to the orderly, and I was immediately told to walk in. The

General rose and greeted me warmly. I expected to see an old, untidy man, and was most agreeably surprised and pleased with his appearance. He is tall, handsome, and powerfully built, but thin. He has brown hair and a brown beard. His mouth expresses great determination. The lips are thin and compressed firmly together; his eyes are blue and dark, with a keen and searching expression. I was told that his age was thirty-eight, and he looks about forty. The General, who is indescribably simple and unaffected in all his ways, took off my wet overcoat with his own hands, made the fire, brought wood for me to put my feet on to keep them warm while my boots were drying, and then began to ask me questions on various subjects. At the dinner-hour we went out and joined the members of his staff. At this meal the General said grace in a fervent, quiet manner, which struck me much. After dinner I returned to his room, and he again talked to me for a long time. The servant came in and took his mattress out of a cupboard and laid it on the floor. As I rose to retire, the General said: 'Captain, there is plenty of room on my bed; I hope you will share it with me.' I thanked him very much for his courtesy, but said, 'Good night,' and slept in a tent, sharing the blankets of one of his aids-de-camp. In the morning, at breakfast-time, I noticed that the General said grace before the meal with the same fervor I had remarked before. An hour or two afterward it was time for me to return to the station; on this occasion, however, I had a horse, and I turned up to the General's quarters to bid him adieu. His room was vacant, so I stepped in and stood before the fire. I then noticed my great-coat stretched before it on a chair. Shortly afterward the General entered the room. He said: 'Captain, I have been trying to dry your great-coat, but I am afraid I have not succeeded very well.' That little act illustrates the man's character. With the cares and responsibilities of a vast army on his shoulders, he finds time to do little acts of kindness and thoughtfulness which make him the darling of his men, who never seem to tire talking of him. Jackson is a man of great endurance ; he drinks nothing stronger than water, and never uses tobacco or any stimulant. He has been known to ride for three days and three nights at a time, and if there is any labor to be undergone, he never fails to take his share of it."

Jackson's appearance on horseback is thus described by a correspondent of the New-York *Tribune :*

"On horseback he by no means looked the hero of a tableau. On his earlier fields and marches he had been blessed with a 'charger' that happily resembled its rider—'a plain horse, that went straight ahead, and minded its own business ;' but one day it got shot under him, and then his friends presented him with a more ornamental beast, a mare that took on airs, and threw him ; so he exchanged her, in disgust, for a less visionary and artistic quadruped—still a horse, but never such a congenial spirit as that original 'Ole Virginny' of his, that never tired, and whose everlasting long-legged, swinging walk was the very thing to make forced marches with. 'He's in the saddle now,' sang those limber Rebels, from the song of their corps :

> 'He's in the saddle now !  Fall in !
>    Steady the whole brigade !
>  Hill's at the Ford, cut off ! we'll win
>    His way out, ball and blade.
>  What matter if our shoes are worn ?
>  What matter if our feet are torn ?
>  Quick-step !  We're with him before morn !
>    That's Stonewall Jackson's way.' "

The following incident in his life is also given by the same correspondent :

"He firmly declined the luxury of 'hospitable mansions' along the line of his march; nor, after his occupation of Winchester, could he, without much difficulty, be induced to pass a night in the house of any old friend in Frederick, Clarke, or Jefferson. He preferred to sleep among his men. It was one of these valley friends of his who miscarried so absurdly in an attempt to cajole him out of his imperturbable reticence. The gentleman, at whose house Jackson had been induced to make a brief visit in passing, was eagerly curious to learn what the next movement of the ubiquitous Rebel would be; so he boldly claimed his confidence on the score of ancient friendship. After a few minutes of well-affected concern and reflection, the grim joker button-holed his bore. 'My staunch old friend,' said he, with mysterious deliberation, 'can—you—keep—a secret?' 'Ah! General.' 'So can I.'"

Jackson's estimation of General Lee is exhibited in the following:

"The love and admiration he at all times evinced for Lee resembled the devotion with which Turner Ashby had followed _him_. Replying to the remarks of a friend about his own peculiar military ideas and habits, and his proneness 'to do his marching and fighting his own way,' he said: 'We are blessed with at least one General whom I would cheerfully follow blindfold, whose most dubious strategy I would execute without question or hesitation, and that General is Robert E. Lee.' The anecdote is authentic. But Jackson had the sagacity to perceive very early that his military genius was essentially local and partisan—that it was as an executive officer exclusively that he was remarkable—and that kaleidoscopic conceptions and subtile combinations must be left to the Lees and Johnstons of the Rebel army."

Sectional hate formed no part of his character, which fact is illustrated in the subjoined anecdote:

"When the question of Secession, Union, or 'Armed Neutrality' went before the people of Virginia, Stonewall Jackson voted the Union ticket; but when the State went out he went with her. From first to last he had no patience (if such a phrase can be true of such a man) with the intemperate expressions of bitter sectional hate that continually affronted his ear; and he was blunt in his admonition to the women of Winchester—when he again left the checkered fortunes of that town to our advancing troops—'not to forget themselves.' 'My child,' he would say to some immoderate Rebel in crinoline, 'you and I have no right to our hates; personal rancor is the lowest expression of patriotism and a sin beside. We must leave these things to God.'"

The author of *Two Months in the Confederate States* relates the following as illustrative of Jackson's devotional habits:

"I was told by the colonel of an artillery regiment, who happened to be encamped in Northern Virginia last summer, close to General Jackson's headquarters, that the general piety of that General, as evidenced by his actions, had not been at all exaggerated. It seems that my friend's tent was so pitched that, from its rear, he commanded a view of the corner of a field, surrounded by a wood, which was not far from Jackson's own tent, but which could be seen by no other persons than those either in my friend's tent or that of General Jackson himself. Twice a day, for weeks, (my friend said,) rain or shine, he saw Jackson slip away to this secluded place—unseen as he believed—and seat himself upon the small fence which bounded the field. There he would remain, often for an hour, with his hands

clasped, face turned upward, convulsed with emotion, the tears
streaming down his face, deep in the performance of secret and agonizing prayer.   Nothing can be said that can increase the value of this
evidence as proving the sincerity of the man."

The religious condition of Jackson's troops is given in
the following extract from a letter written by the Rev. Dr.
Stiles, who was at the time of writing laboring as an evan-
gelist in the Confederate army of the Potomac:

"At his earnest request, I preached to General Pryor's brigade
last Sabbath.   Upon one hour's notice he marched up twelve or fifteen hundred men, who listened with so much interest to a long ser-
mon, that I was not surprised to hear of such a beginning of religious
interest in various regiments of the brigade as issued in a half-way
promise on my part to fall in with the proposal of the General to
preach very early to his soldiers for a succession of nights.   In General Lawton's brigade there is a more decided state of religious excitement.   The great body of the soldiers in some of the regiments
meet for prayer and exhortation every night, exhibit the deepest
solemnity, and present themselves numerously for the prayers of the
chaplains and the Church.   Quite a pleasant number express hope
in Christ.   In all other portions of General Early's division, (formerly General Ewell's,) a similar religious sensibility prevails.

"In General Trimble's, and the immediately neighboring brigades,
there is in progress, at this hour, one of the most glorious revivals
I ever witnessed.   Some days ago a young chaplain of the Baptist
Church—as a representative three others of the same denomination—took a long ride to solicit my coöperation, stating that a promising seriousness had sprung up within their diocese.   I have now
been with him three days and nights, preaching and laboring con-

stantly with the soldiers when not on drill. The audiences and the interest have grown to glorious dimensions. It would rejoice you over-deeply to glance for one instant on our night-meeting in the wild woods, under a full moon, aided by the light of our side-stands. You would behold a mass of men seated on the earth all around you, (I was going to say for the space of half an acre,) fringed in all its circumference by a line of standing officers and soldiers, two or three deep, all exhibiting the most solemn and respectful earnestness that an assembly ever displayed. An officer said to me, last night, on returning from worship, he never had witnessed such a scene, though a Presbyterian elder, especially such an abiding solemnity and delight in the services as prevented all whispering in the outskirts, leaving of the congregation, or restless change of position. I suppose, at the close of the services, we had some sixty or seventy men and officers come forward and publicly solicit an interest in our prayers, and there may have been as many more who from the press could not reach the stand. I have already conversed with quite a number, who seem to give pleasant evidence of a return to God, and all things seem to be rapidly developing for the best.

"The officers, especially Generals Jackson and Early, have modified military rules for our accommodation. I have just learned that General A. P. Hill's division enjoys as rich a dispensation of God's spirit as General Early's. Ask all the brethren and sisters to pray for us and the army at large."

A correspondent of the Savannah *News* portrays General Jackson in the following characteristic sketch:

"There you see self-command, perseverance, indomitable will, that seem neither to know nor think of any earthly obstacle, and all this without the least admixture of vanity, assumption, pride, foolhardiness, or any thing of the kind. There seems a disposition to assert its pretensions, but from the quiet sense of conviction of his relative position, which sets the vexed question of self-importance at rest—a peculiarity, I would remark, of great minds. It is only the little and the frivolous who are forever obtruding their petty vanities before the world. His face also expresses courage in the highest degree, and his phrenological developments indicate a vast amount of energy and activity. His forehead is broad and prominent, the occipital and sincipital regions are both large and well balanced; eyes expressing a singular union of mildness, energy, and concentration; cheek and nose both long and well formed. His dress is a common gray suit of faded cassimere—coat, pants, and hat—the coat slightly braided on the sleeve, just enough to be perceptible, the collar displaying the mark of a Major-General. Of his gait, it is sufficient to say that he just goes along—not a particle of the strut, the military swagger, turkey-gobbler parade, so common among officers of small rank and smaller minds. It would be a profitable study for some of our military swells to devote one hour each day to the contemplation of the magnificent plainness of 'Stonewall.' To military fame which they can never hope to attain he unites the simplicity of a child and the straightforwardness of a Western farmer. There may be those who would be less struck with his appearance as thus accoutred than if bedizened with lace and holding the reins of a magnificent barb caparisoned and harnessed for glorious war; but to one who had seen him, as I had, at Coal Harbor and Malvern Hill, in the rain of shell and the blaze of the death-lights of the battle-field, when nothing less than a mountain would serve as a breastwork against the thirty-six inch shells which howled and shrieked through the sickly air, General Jackson in tatters would be the same hero as General Jackson in gilded uniform. In my simple view he is a nonpareil—he is without a peer. He has enough energy to supply a whole manufacturing district, enough military genius to stock two or three military schools of the size of West-Point."

Dr. Charles Mackay, the New-York correspondent of the (London) *Times*, sketches the great Confederate General in the following terms:

"The interest excited by this strange man is as curious as it is unprecedented. A classmate of McClellan at West-Point, and there considered slow and heavy, unfavorably known in Washington as a hypochondriac and *malade imaginaire*, he has exhibited for the last ten months qualities which were little supposed to reside in his rugged and unsoldierlike frame, but which will hand his name down for many a generation in the company of those great captains whom men will not willingly let die. More apt for the execution than conception of great movements, leaning upon General Lee as the directing brain, and furnishing the promptest hand, the most dauntless heart, the most ascetic and rigorous self-denial, the greatest rapidity and versatility of movement, as his contributions toward the execution of General Lee's strategy, his recent operations in turning General Pope's right, and passing with a force believed not to exceed thirty thousand men to the rear of such an army, massed close to its base of operations and in the act of receiving daily large reënforcements, command universal wonder and admiration. It is said that, like Hannibal, he is accustomed to live among his men without distinction of dress, without greater delicacy of fare, and that it is almost impossible, on this account, for a stranger to recognize or distinguish him among them. Every despatch from his hand has, as its exordium: 'By the blessing of God.' Continual are the prayer-meetings which he holds among his men, invoking a blessing upon his arms before the battle and returning thanks for preservation, and (as it has rarely failed to happen) for victory after it is over.

In fact, they who have seen and heard him uplift his voice in prayer, and then have witnessed his vigor and prompt energy in the strife, say that once again Cromwell is walking the earth and leading his trusting and enraptured hosts to assured victory.  It is not necessary to add that Jackson's men idolize and trust their leader enthusiastically, and have the most implicit faith in his conduct, otherwise the bold and daring steps which he has frequently taken, and from which he has never failed to come off triumphantly, would have been utter impossibilities."

In this connection, the *Saturday Review* (London) says :

" General Jackson's powers of endurance were certainly equalled by his dash and daring.  Less than two years fill up his public life, and not much more than twelve months complete the cycle of his leading victories ; but he compressed into the narrow space of two campaigns as many triumphs as have distinguished the long military life of several famous captains.  Although not the general-in-chief of an army, not a few of his successes were won in an independent command, and as many as six great victories are attributed to Jackson.  . . .  His religion, though it may not be our religion, was not inconsistent with charity, gentleness, and courtesy ; and the victorious general who is a high-minded gentleman, a consistent Christian, and whose popularity is universal among his men, is not, after all, a very common character.  The military profession wants such bright and rare reliefs ; and we will venture to say that throughout England, and even among the better spirits of the Federals, there is a general share in that ' deep grief' with which the South may well mourn the death of Lieutenant-General Jackson.  There is something of a national sympathy with those simple and touching words with which General Lee records ' the daring, skill, and energy of this great and good soldier,' and asks his comrades, 'while they mourn his death, to feel that his spirit lives, and will inspire the whole army with his indomitable courage and unshaken confidence in God as their hope and strength.' "

The New-York *Independent* criticises Jackson's character and career from a Northern stand-point, as follows:

" We are in some respects better judges of his military talents than Southern men, since we felt the blows which they only saw dealt. It is certain that no other man has impressed the imagination of our soldiers and the whole community so much as he. An unknown name at the beginning of the war, save to his brother officers, and to his classes in the military school at Lexington, Virginia, his footsteps were earliest in the field from which now death has withdrawn them. But in two years he has made his name familiar in every civilized land on the globe as a general of rare skill, resource, and energy.

" No other general of the South could develop so much power out of slender and precarious means, by the fervid inspiration of his own mind, as Jackson. He had absolute control of his men, seeming almost to fascinate them. He drove them through marches long and difficult, without resources, feeding them as best he could; he delivered battles as a thunder-cloud discharged bolts, and, if the fortunes were against him, then, with even more remarkable skill than in advancing, he held his men together in retreat; and with extraordinary address and courage, eluded pursuit, sometimes fighting, sometimes fleeing, till he brought off his forces safely. Then, almost before the dust was laid upon the war-path, his face was again toward his enemies, and he was ready for renewed conflict. His whole soul was in his work. He had no doubts nor parleyings within himself. He put the whole force of his being into his blows for the worst cause man ever fought for, as few of our generals have ever learned to do for the best cause for which trumpet ever sounded. Henceforth we know him no more after the flesh. He is no longer a foe. We think of him now as a noble-minded gentleman, a rare and eminent Christian! For years he has been an active member of the Presbyterian Church, of which he was a ruling elder. He never, in all the occupations of the camp, or temptation of campaigns, lost the fervor of his piety, or remitted his Christian duties.

"We know that before every important move he spent much time in prayer. He had so put his soul in the keeping of his Master, that he was relieved from all thought of self, and had the whole power of his life ready for his work. Officers of Fremont's army, who pursued him in his famous retreat from the Shenandoah Valley, found him to be greatly beloved by the common people, among whom, in former times, he had labored, in prayer-meetings, in temperance-meetings, and in every Christian word and work. No wonder he fought well along a region whose topography he had mapped down with prayers, exhortations, and Christian labor!

"He was unselfish. He fought neither for reputation now, nor for future personal advancement. . . . He incessantly struck on the right and on the left, and kept alive the fire in the hearts of ill-clad, poorly-fed, and over-worked men by the excitement of enterprise and the constant relish of victories, small in detail, but whose sum was all-important. Let no man suppose that the North will triumph over a fallen son with insulting gratulations! Nowhere else will the name of Jackson be more honored."

www.ingramcontent.com/pod-product-compliance
Lightning Source LLC
Chambersburg PA
CBHW020106030726
47498CB00006B/1971